Manipulating Fate

Angela Lantzy

PublishAmerica
Baltimore

© 2004 by Angela Lantzy.
All rights reserved. No part of this book may be reproduced, stored in a retrieval system or transmitted in any form or by any means without the prior written permission of the publishers, except by a reviewer who may quote brief passages in a review to be printed in a newspaper, magazine or journal.

First printing

ISBN: 1-4137-1121-9
PUBLISHED BY PUBLISHAMERICA, LLLP
www.publishamerica.com
Baltimore

For my best friend and biggest supporter, my husband Scott,
who has the wisdom to understand me
and the patience to let me follow my
dreams.

ACKNOWLEDGMENTS

This book would have never happened if it weren't for a some very special people. My mother, Ginny Snyder, the first person to read what I had written. Your encouragement and faith in me was what kept me going. Jennie Zacharyasz, without your editing, thoughts and ideas, this book would still be just a file in my computer. Paul Oberth, I couldn't have 'murdered' without you. My sister, Jeanne Reihl. No matter how bizarre my thoughts, you always listened and never questioned my sanity. Everyone at Baldwin-Wallace College who read bits and pieces of this novel in progress. Thanks for bearing with me for eight months.

I'd also like to say thank you to my photographer, Mike Brahm. What I considered an unpleasant task, you made fun. Thanks. Mahler Museum in Berea. A great place and the perfect background for my pictures. The City of Berea, which in 1836, on the flip of a coin, chose the name Berea over Tabor. Berea is a wonderful city, rich in history, and inspiration for this book. And last but not least, Publish America, thank you for taking a chance on this book and completing my dream.

PROLOGUE

The late September air was crisp even by northeast Ohio standards. With no clouds to blanket in the warmth of the day, the temperature this night was around 42 degrees. The trees were just beginning their transformation from green to the reds and oranges of fall. Even in the early twilight, he could see the late night sky would be chock full of stars. It would provide the perfect opportunity. The moon was glowing bright already. Except for the smallest fraction of a sliver, it would have been full. This gave him ample light for the work ahead. He could not have planned a better evening.

Following her into the park, he'd watched patiently as she settled on a bench with a cup of hot chocolate and a book. Text book reading judging by the thickness of it. He had walked onto the path after twenty minutes with a blanket in one hand and a bottle of wine in the other. She looked up as he approached and smiled. Stopping, he smiled and began to chat about the weather. Curiosity got the best of her and it didn't take long before she asked where he was headed. Alcohol wasn't permitted in state parks so he told her about a private little spot in the woods off the beaten path, which had a large clearing. He sometimes went there to be closer to nature, drink some wine and on clear nights like this, count the stars.

Her smile had broadened till all her straight, white teeth could be seen. Her blonde hair fell back as she tilted her head skyward. A short, soft laugh escaped her as she commented how much better that sounded than reading short stories for her American Lit class. He knew the quest for an invitation would come, so he'd asked if she'd like to join him. It was all too easy. Something from a recipe book: One blanket, one bottle of cheap wine, one good-looking guy, and one young, blonde, naive college girl. Mix in reclusive spots and stars. Spread on charm; bask in moonlight for thirty minutes. Kill when ready.

He smiled at his own humor. He doubted she'd find it as amusing. She didn't have a clue to what was to come. They got to the clearing and spread the thick blanket out. He pulled out a red, disposable plastic cup from his jacket and poured the wine. They sat together, sharing the cup, gazing at the stars, and talking about her insignificant dreams for the future. He wanted to laugh and tell her she had no future but, instead, leaned over to kiss her. She responded with a passion. It took ten minutes til he had her undressed down to her navy blue Victoria Secret's Wonder Bra and matching panties. Her eyes had widened in confusion when he pulled out the nylon rope. Horror gripped her when she saw the rock he held. He hit her hard in the left temple but not too hard. He wanted her dazed and unsteady but conscious.

The memory and his final act left him grinning ear to ear. Alone in the woods now, he could hear a deer rustling around in the distance. The air was damp, the smell of wet earth and leaves were heavy but still the other scents lingered. The act had required some exertion that left his skin covered with a fine sheen of sweat that could still be detected. The metallic scent of blood was there but the most prevalent above the earthen smell was that of fear. He had seen it in her eyes, saw her muscles tighten so hard she began to shake all over. The tears flowed, then the begging to spare her life and finally the prayers to an all-merciful god to save her. Yes, fear had a scent and he was dancing in it.

His hands ached a little from the nylon rope he'd used to strangle her. The most difficult part was tying her up. He'd come to this spot a week earlier to leave extra rope along with the smaller piece he'd killed her with. Dead leaves covered the forest floor and hiding the rope was quite easy. The thought that some kid playing down here would find them never worried him. He deserved his reward. The gloves saved him from any marks but whatever pain he suffered was worth it. It was a labor of love for him. Like a cat bringing home a dead mouse or bird to its owner; the girl was a gift. A gift for the woman he loved and longed to make his. Eventually, Kori Chandler would know him better than anyone ever would. They would have the perfect love, the perfect life. She would see him for all his glory.

But first, she would see the gift.
He was almost done here. All that was left do was pin the note to his new friend.

CHAPTER 1

Kori Chandler discovered two things about herself early in life. First, she was not a morning person. Second, she hated the beeping of an alarm clock. She bought a radio/alarm clock once and set the wake-up to music. The only thing that did was put a sound track to her dreams.

She rolled out of bed at seven in the morning with a moan. To her, Sunday was meant for sleeping. Fall was settling in and the mornings were becoming a little darker than a month ago, which was not helping her mood at all. Normally, Kori hibernated till at least 10 a.m. or later, but her best friend Paige McCleary had asked her to help paint the living room of Paige's newly acquired house.

Stumbling down the steps, Kori headed for the kitchen. The new Bunn coffee machine was waiting patiently for her. This morning, coffee would be her lifeline. Harley, her golden retriever, was lying by the back door. She let him out and started the vanilla nut coffee brewing. While the aroma filtered through the kitchen and eventually, the rest of the house, she headed for the bathroom.

One look in the mirror and she knew she was lucky Paige was the only one who'd see her this morning. Kori smiled to the reflection but still the tiredness showed. Her shoulder length chestnut hair hung limply around her face. She could see stray hairs sticking up in the back giving the impression she'd spent the night on her back shaking her head no. The dark circles weren't doing anything for the image either. And she swore she saw two new lines by her mouth when she smiled.

Turning thirty this past March wasn't actually the highlight of her life. Her mother had called her first thing that day and sang happy birthday which she didn't appreciate at six o'clock in the morning. But she did have a great house she bought a year and a half ago, owned a small coffee shop in the middle of downtown Tabor, plenty of good friends and a loyal dog.

As she made her way back to the kitchen and the saving grace of caffeine, she recalled the next thing out of her mother's mouth was asking how much longer Kori planned to wait before getting married and making her a grandmother. She swore to herself right there she'd never do that to her children. Of course, that statement would make her mother happy because it implied Kori would get around to having kids.

She was about to go out front and get the morning paper when she noticed Harley was still standing on the porch. It had always been his custom to charge down the steps, bound across the back yard and head for the woods that was the property line. But, there he was, still on the porch. He turned his head when she opened the door. "What's the problem this morning Harley? Are you waiting for an invite from the squirrels?" It was a beautiful clear day, though a bit nippy for her. Bulky, white clouds had rolled in spotting the light blue sky and birds were singing, which is when she noticed something on the tree at the end of the yard. " What is that boy?" But the dog only whimpered and bowed his head.

Kori returned to the kitchen, slipped on tennis shoes, and grabbed her jacket. "Come on boy, let's go see what's down there." Her property stretched about fifty yards from the back of the house to the beginning of the woods. The land sloped a bit but the size and knowledge that a house wouldn't be built directly behind her was the selling point for her. She crossed the first twenty yards with Harley right behind her, with a mindset of curiosity. She knew local kids played in the woods but she'd never had a problem with any of them. She could see something on one of the trees but couldn't quite make out what it was.

Another ten yards and it began to take shape but made no sense. It almost looked like a woman, but, no, it couldn't be. Her pace slowed as curiosity left her and uncertainty began to take hold. A couple of more steps and, oh god, it was. She could feel her heart pounding, the rush of blood in her ears drowned out any birds that may have been singing. There was something stuck to her chest but Kori couldn't see what it was. She didn't want to know. What she wanted to do was scream like she never had but when her mouth opened only a strangled gasp came out. She wanted to turn away and run but her legs felt as though they'd give out if she moved.

Harley barked once and brought her out that dizzying fall of disbelief. Kori finally turned and began to run back to the house. It felt as if her legs were two concrete pillars and she was running in quicksand. Two minutes seemed more like twenty. She reached the door, got Harley in, slammed and locked it. Collapsing onto a chair she tried to pull herself together. The police had to be called.

"911. What's your emergency?"

"There's a dead body in my yard." It sounded so absurd she wondered if they'd believe her.

"What's the address?"

"Seventy-five Maple Lane." How could that woman sound so calm? Did people call in with this problem every day? Kori hung up. They knew her address and probably her number as well. If they thought she was some crackpot they could just call back.

The police arrived within 10 minutes. In that time, she'd sufficiently worked herself to the brink of hysteria. She caught a glimpse of herself in the oval mirror hung by the front door. Her hair looked more disheveled than she'd started with, circles under her eyes darkened to the shade of a ripe plum, and her blue eyes were bloodshot from crying. Her eyes worried her. They screamed woman -on- the- verge- of -a -breakdown. Had she realized all this before the police arrived, she'd have tried to do something with herself.

Not being vane, simply worried they might think she was the psycho tying people up.

By eight thirty, her house was the neighborhood attraction. Four police cars had shown up at this point along with an unmarked car and a van. Police had cordoned off the woods, removed the body from the tree and began a search of the surrounding area for evidence. Detective Bakker was still questioning her.

"And you said you got home at what time?"

"3:30a.m."

"And that's usual for a Saturday?"

"Yes. We like to get a live band in on Saturday nights. By the time we clean up, the band packs, money is paid to the talent and cash is counted it's late." They'd been over this before. Kori decided the detective liked playing the role of a inquisitive inspector.

Detective Bakker plodded along. "You notice anything different when you arrived home?"

Exhaling slowly, she repeated "No, I did not. The front door was locked. Harley greeted me as always. I didn't see anything out of order or missing. Of course, I didn't go out back either."

"Didn't you let the dog out?"

"Yes. I let him out the front. I always do. Why close one door and then walk all the way to the back door just to let a dog pee." Kori tried to see last night again. She'd been tired but not so that she would have missed any sign of an intruder. That she was certain of. But had Harley been acting normal or was she exhausted to the point of missing his cue? No. He'd been fine. She was sure.

Kori knew Detective Bakker was watching her. He may like playing roles but he wasn't an idiot. He was sizing her up. Not that she could have done this but they both knew this was personal. No sense in kidding herself on that. She heard the detective saying something. "Miss Chandler?"

"I'm sorry. You said something?" Great, now she looked like an idiot.

"Miss Chandler, do you have any idea who would want to do this? Ex-boyfriend, former employee, disputes with a neighbor. Anything would help."

She'd thought about it for some time already. Kori hadn't fired anyone lately and she and the few neighbors she had all got along just fine. That only left Boyd Thomas. They had dated for two years and finally broken it off five months ago. It had been an amicable parting. He was ready for the "settled life"; marriage, kids, nine-to-five work and the very thought of it all scarred the wits out of her. Boyd deserved better so she let go.

Detective Bakker was a patient man. He could see her thinking this through. And this usually meant an old boyfriend floating around.

"Miss Chandler, nobody likes to toss out names when police are investigating a murder but it does give us a starting point. Maybe the person you know has nothing to do with this but they may be able to lead us in the right direction. Perhaps you could give us a list of friends, acquaintances, employees, anyone you have contact with that would have the opportunity to get a view of your habits." That's what he'd prefer. A list of anyone she was around. The note left on the body bothered him. Kori hadn't mentioned seeing a note so he hadn't said a word about it. Yet.

Kori didn't want to drag Boyd into this and in doing so, back into her life. She knew the detective was waiting for her to say something, anything. What he said next sent a chill straight to the core of her being. She knew at that moment, her life would never be the same.

"Miss Chandler. There was a note found on the body. I'd like you to look at it and tell me if you recognize the handwriting or if it has any meaning to you." Kori sat rock still. He slid a small, white piece of paper across the table. How long had they been here? It seemed like several hours but couldn't have been more than two. It was taking on the feel of a bad movie. It didn't feel like her kitchen any longer but just a set for a movie. This couldn't be her life.

As she glanced down, she could see the stain of blood on the paper, the hole where something once held it to the woman. She was cold and as she read the note, the feeling intensified. Her hands were shaking and breathing was becoming hard work. Written in perfect, half-inch block letters were the two sentences: Because I could not stop for Death—he Kindly stopped for me. "I don't recognize the handwriting." Though she'd heard it many times before.

Thursday night at the coffee shop was poetry night. Some poets were quite dramatic and somber and therefore were drawn to this poem. "I'm familiar with the words. They're from a poem by Emily Dickinson. She never titled her poems so they're known by the first sentence. She also never used proper grammar or punctuation."

"So is this the way it would appear in a book of poetry?" The detective had the thoughtful, inquisitive look about him again but Kori had the impression he already knew the answers to his questions.

"I believe it would be. I think the rest of the stanza continues: 'The carriage held but just ourselves—and immortality.' I've heard it and seen it before but never really studied it. It means nothing to me personally. You'd have to ask an English Professor for the exact meaning."

"I'll keep that in mind, Miss Chandler." With that, Detective Bakker stood and thanked her for her cooperation. He gave her his card with every conceivable way of contacting him on it, said he'd be in touch and not to hesitate to call him.

After hours with police officers walking in and out, the house had an eerily quiet sensation. She and Harley stared at one another for a moment both lost in their own thoughts. She couldn't imagine what the poor dog must be thinking and had the idea she didn't want to know. "Well, I guess I'd better make a phone call to Boyd." Harley only tilted his head and continued to stare.

That's when she remembered Paige. Curiously, she wondered why she hadn't tried to call her. She checked the caller I.D. display and saw she had called at seven thirty-two. She must have been on the Alice in Wonderland walk in the back yard. She dialed Paige's number. Four rings and still no answer. Kori wondered why she hadn't called back. Two more rings and nothing. Must be into the painting. Finally, she picked up.

"Hello?"

"Paige, it's me. I don't think I'm going to be painting today." She felt both physically and mentally drained.

" I figured that. Not every day a dead body shows up in the yard. That's horrible. Any idea who it is?"

Kori was surprised. Not by the fact Paige already knew about the day's news but the nonchalant way she approached the subject. She vaguely recalled the 911 operator who spoke with the same detachment. Of course, that was the operator's job.

"No but how did you find out so fast though?"

"Gabe said he wasn't busy today so he offered his painter's touch. I said you were coming and I asked if he'd mind picking you up on his way over. I called and when you didn't answer he said he'd swing by anyway and see if any lights were on yet. But when he got there the street was lined with police cars and the good people of the neighborhood. He stopped and asked some guy what was up."

"Paige, who's Gabe?"

"My house painter. Well, exterior house painter. He moved here about six months ago from Cleveland and started up his own business. Kinda like a handyman thing, does house painting, landscaping, knows some plumbing and electrical. Just the kind of guy you need to hire when you're married to Matt."

Matt McCleary was the nicest guy you ever wanted to meet but absolutely clueless when it came fixing anything. He was an accountant and if you needed anything except a calculator fixed forget asking him. Kori had been amazed they'd bought a house in the first place. Apartment dwellers seemed the best way to describe Matt and Paige. But to each their own. She couldn't see Paige with anybody else.

She and Paige had met in fifth grade. They had their fights and disagreements but in the end, their friendship had survived. Paige hadn't changed much over the years. Always determined, persistent, a little self-centered, and never shy. There had been a time when Kori had planned for college, marriage, the whole works and Paige had stood by her, flatly refusing to believe any of it. She considered Kori and herself "free spirits". No man or business would hold them down or tell them what to do. Just to prove her wrong, Kori enrolled at Tabor College. It only lasted a year but by her standards, that was pretty good. She'd fallen in love with a budding local musician and at the end of the semester they ran off and got married. That only lasted six months.

"I'll try and stop over later. I think Harley and I need to get out for a while. Nice long walk might do us both some good about now." Along with a long hot bath and a bottle of wine but that could wait till a respectable hour. Wouldn't want to become a lush just yet in life.

"Whatever. We'll be painting through the night at the pace we're going. Matt's going to have a cow when he gets home though."

"Where'd he run off to on a Sunday morning?"

"No clue. Heard you were coming and ran out of here." She was laughing. Matt knew painting wasn't Kori's forte in life. He'd seen her paint before in her own house and had commented once that she had more paint on her than the walls.

"Thanks. That makes me feel so much better." Kori smiled anyway. It was hard not too.

In Paige's world, if it didn't directly affect her, it couldn't be all that bad. Dead bodies included.

"Hey, you planning on stopping by the coffee shop?"

"The thought crossed my mind. Just to make sure every thing is running smoothly." Though she new it would be. Sunday's weren't very hectic and Janine Crawler was very competent. That was the best choice she'd make in ages hiring her.

Janine was younger than she but was dependable, hard working, and had a genuine love of people.

"Cool. How 'bout picking up a couple caramel lattes and bring them with you?"

"I think I can manage that"

"Oh. Think you could make that a double shot too. I'm going to need the caffeine jolt to finish this project today."

"I'll be there about six."

"Thanks."

Before she and Harley headed out the door Kori needed to finish two tasks and neither one was appealing. First, she had to call Boyd. The police had probably already contacted him but she still felt she owed him at least a phone call. Kori gave up on the sixth ring. He'll just have to wait. The second item on the agenda was to do something with herself so she didn't scare unsuspecting customers or unknowing bystanders.

Taking Harley for a walk was the best idea Kori had all day. She had figured everyone in town must know about the body by now so she hadn't focused too much on her appearance. The hair was unsalvageable and had to be washed. She worried a brush would get lost in the mess she'd had on her head. She added a little blush, some lipstick, threw on a pair of jeans and an old Tabor College sweatshirt and off they went. It had turned out to be a gorgeous fall day. The leaves were turning in a fury of color making sure no one missed the arrival of fall.

She'd decided to head south on Maple. It was one of the most breath-taking of the six streets named after the trees that lined the yards and tree lawns. Beech, Hickory, Chestnut, and Maple were sandwiched between Buckeye and Oak. Oak Parkway was the newest and the four side streets all ended into it. Kori turned left onto Oak and headed toward the new development.

Someone in city planning must have gotten bored one day. Woods ran the entire back length of all the houses on Maple. A land bridge separated the woods from Tabor Lake. The lake was actually created from digging out sandstone from the earth over a century ago. It was then filled with water from a trench dug from a river that ran through the city. The land bridge had once been the route trains had followed steaming the sandstone north to Cleveland. Since only a small section of trees blocked Oak Parkway from the land bridge, city planners cut through the woods, extended Oak and opened up a large track of land that wasn't being used.

Kori and Harley walked across the bridge and into the new housing development. Since houses backed up to a view of the lake, a small wooded path was kept for people to walk on. The path was paved and wrapped around the lake and into the small downtown area of Tabor. Main Street was the largest in downtown with four small streets bisecting it. Small shops lined Main Street. Everything you needed could be found there. It had the look and feel of a small, cozy town but extremely functional. If you wanted Wal-Mart though, you had to drive a quick fifteen minutes into Newton Falls.

The stores where all built in the late 1800's out of red brick and sandstone. The bottom half was commercial and the upper floors were mostly converted into one and two bedroom apartments. There were twenty-four shops altogether and the varieties ran the gamut. Whatever you could imagine was there. Stores lined both sides of

Main and ran in sections of four per block. The streets that divided the sections were lined with some of the oldest homes in Tabor. When she bought the building that now housed Kori's Koffee, she had lived upstairs for three years. Sometimes she really missed the convenience of it but she loved her house. At least she felt she could get away from work now and then.

Kori's Koffe was in the middle of Main Street. The used bookstore Paige owned was one section before her cafe. She smiled every time she saw the sign for her cafe. Kori had been sad at the passing of her grandmother but equally shocked to find her grandmother was quite wealthy. Catherine Chandler never had the usual knick-knacks you find in other homes. Her grandmother's motto was if it didn't have a function, why bother. Kori guessed the money other people spent on souvenirs and decorations, Catherine just hoarded away. Catherine had bequeathed her enough to buy the building out-right.

Kori lead Harley up the separate entrance to the old apartment. She though about renting the one bedroom apartment but reconsidered. It made a great office and added more storage space. Getting a fresh bowl of water for Simon, she left him there and headed into the cafe. As usual, all was running well. Janine was at the bar where two customers sat sipping espresso. A couple was at one end of the store having an animated conversation. Janine smiled when she saw Kori come in.

"Hi. I heard about your morning. How you holding up?"

Kori smiled back and sighed. News does travel fast. Tabor is basically a college town now. On a good day, it's home to about five thousand people. He personal belief was that the city did its count in August when the kids came back to school.

"I'm fine. I just hope they catch whoever did this fast. I don't want this to drag out. And I hope they find out who that woman was and her parents survive this."

"I'm trying not to think about it. That poor girl must have been scarred shitless."

Janine gave a little shudder. "Oh. Before I forget, Elliot was in here looking for you. He knew you probably wouldn't be in yet but said he had some papers to go over and was headed to his office if you wanted to stop by."

"Did he hear what happened?"

"Not until I told him. Figured he'd hear about it anyway so it might as well come from me. You could see he's worried but you know him. He just pressed his lips together and shook his head. At least call him if you not going to see him. I told him I'd at least make sure you'd call."

Well, if there had been any doubt about seeing Elliot today, Janine just solved it.

Kori knew one of Janine's pet peeves was people saying one thing and doing another. She made a promise for you, you were damn well going to keep it. Kori simply smiled. It wasn't as though Janine had to twist her arm to go see Elliot. She'd do that for the sheer joy of seeing him.

Elliot Bowman was an English professor at Tabor College. He lived here for all but eight years while he attended college but they had just met four months ago. She'd seen him come into the cafe before and had exchanged pleasantries with him but it wasn't until he started coming to poetry nights that they became friends. He got wind that some of his students would read original poetry and he'd come to see them.

He had such a quiet, unassuming way about him; she was hooked the first time they had a long conversation. Elliot was fifty but she hardly noticed the twenty year age difference. Only when they discussed music or fashion trends of their youth did the years become apparent. His hair was gray flecked with black rather than vice versa. Elliot reached the six-foot mark so she had to tilt her head a few degrees to be able to see his best feature, his eyes. It sounded corny just thinking about it. But his eyes were a shade of blue that left you wondering if they weren't really white with a little color thrown in. They had a mesmerizing effect on her. Like he could see right through her and she didn't mind a bit.

Kori hadn't heard one student complain about his classes. It wasn't that his was an easy class that you could simply coast through, he just engaged them enough to get their brains moving without overtaxing them. He'd come in every Thursday night for six weeks before he asked her to dinner. She smiled just thinking about that night. They'd decided on Tommy's Bar and Grill. It wasn't far from the college and it had a friendly atmosphere. Not large or small, it had five booths that lined the back and about fifteen tables filling in the rest of the space. The bar had approximately twelve stools, which were well worn. Two large television sets were mounted to the wall behind the bar and it was easy to imagine the "regulars" coming in to watch the Cleveland Browns play football on Sundays.

The only word she could think of to describe that evening was charming. He'd picked her up at eight o'clock. The evening lasted till one in the morning. From the ride to the restaurant, through dinner, a walk, and escorting her to the front door, they never stopped talking. She'd learned that night he'd been married twenty years when his wife was diagnosed with stomach cancer. Elliot suggested going to the doctor but she was convinced it was simply an ulcer. By the time she discovered the real problem it was too late. From time of diagnosis to the day she died took five months.

Elliot told Kori he and his wife tried to have children but never did. After she died, he threw himself into his work and was just now starting to see the world around him. They talked about her year at Tabor and his teaching, their careers, family and friends. Kori knew as she crawled into bed that night that even if things didn't turn romantic with him, she wanted to be a friend for life.

The clanging of bells against the cafe door brought Kori back to the here and now. It was already three o'clock. If she was going to the college to see Elliot and still make it to Paige's by six, she'd better get moving. She figured she could walk over to the college, see Elliot, and shoot back to the cafe for Harley and the latte's and then head to Paige's. Well, she didn't have anything else better to do except think about today and that was the last thing she wanted to ponder.

Deer Lane bisected Main Street in the middle. Heading down Deer, she would run right into Center Street, which was the next main avenue in Tabor, and the street where Tabor College's main campus stood. The day had started out cold but had warmed to sixty degree's by the time Kori started walking. At the end of Deer, she turned right on Center. The next two blocks were lined with five small buildings built anywhere from 1880 to 1886. Again, they consisted of bricks and sandstone, but these building, housed classrooms and each one held a few offices of the professors.

Elliot Bowman's office was located on the third floor of the first building. Kori loved walking into the old buildings. It appealed to her fascination with history. Sometimes she would try and imagine all the people who had walked through these halls. What it must have been like to be a woman, say in the early twentieth century, attending college.

The walls were painted pale beige and the carpet was what she could only call tweed. She had once laughed that Elliot should be careful not to fall because he owned a tweed jacket almost the exact shade of the carpet. The kids would just walk right over him. He laughed but refused to part with the jacket. Elliot believed every English professor in a small, private college needed to own one.

The windows she passed always amazed her. They must be at least five feet tall. They started out wide at the base but came to a point at the top giving them a look that belonged more on an old church cathedral than a college building. In a time before electricity she supposed you needed large windows.

Sometimes the halls seemed too quiet. The old steam radiators clinked as the water heated and expanded the pipes. A light musty smell still hung around despite new carpet and paint through the years. She'd heard the ghost stories that must be a requirement for these types of building but it was in these quiet moments when kids were in class or gone for the day, that she almost believed them.

She could almost feel the spirit of the girl who supposedly killed herself in the early 1900's because she'd found out she was pregnant. Or the wandering ghost of a boy sent to school to become a doctor. He supposedly was horsing around on the third floor, fell over the railing and dropped three stories to his death. Kori was only too happy to reach Elliot's door. After a day like she's had, thinking about dead students haunting Tabor was not a good idea. She was beginning to rattle herself again.

She leaned against the doorjamb watching him. Kori would have never believed someone could use this hole-in-the-wall as an office. Elliot had managed to fit in a desk and chair, an old green, leather couch, a chair for visitors, and line the rest of the walls with bookcases, in an area better described as a broom closet. She smiled and said hi.

As he turned at the sound of her voice, she was once again aware of the physical attraction she had for him. After three months, he had just begun to hold her hand and kiss her on the cheek at the end of an evening out. Gentleman were nice but she had the feeling she wouldn't mind seeing the bad-boy image of Elliot Bowman. She had only taken one step inside the door and he still reached her with two steps on his part.

"Hi. I heard about the murder. How are you holding up?"

"Okay. I'll survive. I feel awful for the poor girl and her family. Thinking about what they'll go through I guess I don't have much to complain about. But the idea someone did this to get my attention is sick. What kind of human being does something like that? Who thinks like that?" She could feel herself getting upset. Her eyes were already glistening with tears. She wasn't going to cry. It sure wasn't going to help . But by the time she finished her sentence, Elliot was already wrapping his arms around her. She could feel the steady beat of his heart and the warmth coming from his body. He kissed the top of her head and hugged her a little tighter. She could smell the distinct scent of Old Spice. This is exactly what she needed. For the first time since finding the woman, she felt safe and secure.

"Kori there are a lot of sick people in this world. Don't start blaming yourself. If this guy left a body for you to find, he's just sick. You didn't bring this on yourself."

"Do you know he left a note on her? He quoted Emily Dickinson. How nuts can you be if you can quote her? I don't know. I just hate the thought that I had anything to do with this."

"Kori, we both know Dickinson's work isn't unheard of. Kids can be introduced to select poems by her at the eight-grade level. Not to mention through high school and college."

"It's just creepy to think some guy thought all this out and then did it. You have to wonder why there wasn't something in his brain screaming for him to stop. Like, 'hey, you know this is sick and deranged!'"

"Which poem did he use anyway?"

"Because I could not stop for death. Crazy."

"If you're really worried, you could stay with me till they figure out who did this."

She almost dropped on the floor. That was the last thing she would ever have thought he'd say. It's not that he didn't care for her but she always got the impression he liked his own space. She'd been to his townhouse before. He lived in the new development she had walked Harley around to get to the coffee shop. The first time she went over there, her first thought was that he either had an obsessive/compulsive cleanliness disorder or he didn't spend a lot of time there. Kori couldn't see herself there. She'd probably be more nervous about breaking his routine, whatever it may be, than staying in her house.

"Thanks but I'll be fine. It's not like he left the woman in my kitchen. It was fifty yards away. Technically, not even on my property. Plus, I've got Harley. I don't think he'd let anyone in the house and I hope he'd bark his head off if a stranger got close to the house."

"Well, don't rely solely on a dog. When you go home, make sure all the windows and doors are locked, okay?"

"Yes. I already checked the windows before I left today. I'll be fine Elliot."

"Would you like to have dinner with me?"

"Can I take a rain check? I promised Paige I'd stop over about six. Originally, we were supposed to paint but I never made it. Thought I'd see if I could help any tonight. Keep my mind occupied."

"Definitely take a rain check. You are planning to drive over so you're not walking in the dark aren't you?"

"Yes. I have to go back to the cafe and get Harley and Paige's latte, and then I'll go home and get my car. You're starting to sound like my father, you know. Anyway, I better get going. If I'm late, Paige will start to worry and I wouldn't want that many people to get worked up in one day."

"All right. I wouldn't want Paige to fret over you. Might throw off her entire schedule for the evening."

Kori laughed. She and Elliot had spent many nights in the company of Paige and he had picked up on her idiosyncrasies almost from the start. "Do me one favor though. Please call me when you get in. I'll feel better knowing you're home safe and sound. All right?"

"I think I can manage that as long as you don't mind late night phone calls. I have a feeling Paige might have me there for a while."

"I don't mind what time it is. Just call me." She smiled and kissed him on the cheek. He seemed to hug her a little tighter and a little longer . They said good-bye and she headed back to the cafe. It felt like it was getting cooler out and she'd be happy to get back to the warmth of a house, be it her house or Paige's. Kori popped her head in the cafe. "Janine?"

"You're back soon. Whatcha need?"

"Could you make two large caramel lattes? Make one a double shot, please. I'm going to grab Harley and I'll be right back."

She ran up the stairs and got Harley's leash. He had been napping on his dog bed but was up in a second when he saw the leash. "Let's roll boy. We still have to walk home and get the car." They stopped for the lattes and started their walk back. Opting for the short route to save some time, she headed down Main Street. Turning right onto Oak she started to feel a little silly. Paige and Matt's house was on Beech Lane. Three streets separated their homes and the thought of walking right past Paige's street so she could get her car and drive over seemed ridiculous. She and Harley could always hit Buckeye, which was a little busier than Oak, to walk home. There were plenty of cars and lights to make her feel safe. Besides, she had Harley.

With that settled, she turned onto Beech. Paige's house was smack in the middle of the street. Carrying two drinks and holding a leash was not an easy feat. She'd be really surprised to make it there without spilling anything much less getting to her house. Why she hadn't thought to grab a carrier for the drinks was beyond her.

Paige's house was in clear view now. It could be a beautiful house with a coat of paint, new roof, and gutters. Matt and Paige said they got one hell of a deal on the four-bedroom colonial and ever time Kori saw it she knew they weren't lying. It surprised her the previous owners hadn't just given it to them. The thought that Paige's interest could be sustained long enough to fix it up just plain shocked her.

She used the back door and walked right into the kitchen. That was a shock to the system too. Kori doubted it had been painted, along with the rest of the house, since the fifties. The entire kitchen was a deep yellow. The walls and ceiling were the same paint color. The floor and counters were a softer shade but still yellow. She figured this is what a bee must see when it lands on a yellow daffodil newly opened in the spring. Kori prayed the daffodil smelled better than this kitchen did right now though.

The aroma of pepperoni and sausage pizza assaulted her first. It was mingled in with the smell of cleaner freshened with pine. And something that smelled like old glue to her. Cans of paint were stacked against one side of the kitchen and she carefully maneuvered around brushes, rolls of plastic and garbage bags. And then she saw Paige in the doorway. Kori laughed so hard she thought she was going to wet herself. She'd never seen Paige look so disheveled in all the years she'd known her.

"Thank you. You look lovely too."

"I'm sorry Paige. It's just that I've never seen you with a bandana on your head."

"Is that all or would you like to continue? I wouldn't want to ruin your fun."

"Well, if you'll allow, the coverall thing doesn't really work for you. I don't think I've ever seen you barefoot or with paint and dirt all over your face either." By now, even Paige was smiling. This was one of the images in life she'd never forget.

"If you're done now, would you like to see what I've done so far?"

"Sure. Lead the way beautiful. Has Matt seen you yet?"

"No and he never will. I'm headed to the shower right after you see the living room."

"You never did say where he went today."

"Oh, his mother's of course. She must have burned out a light bulb or something stupid."

Paige and Matt's mother, Susan had never gotten along to put it mildly. Paige had wondered if she'd bother showing up at the wedding and, if she did, thought it would be to boycott it. When they came to the living room it looked totally different. Kori had begun to think the style of the old owners was to paint everything the same and match the surrounding furniture to the color of the walls.

On first seeing the house, the living room was green. Yes, everything. From the walls right down to the shag carpeting and couch that had been left. Now, it was a pale blue with the trim and ceiling done in white. The carpet had also been pulled up and the natural hardwood floors refinished.

"Paige, it gorgeous. It looks like a completely different room." Kori was honestly amazed.

"Originally, I was going to do the trim a darker blue but Gabe said the trim and ceiling both being white might look better, especially if I was going to leave the bookcases.   "I like it this way. Guess this guy does know something about painting."

"Gabe is terrific. Very handy, very patient, and very good-looking."

"You are married Paige."

"Doesn't mean I can't look. Besides, I was thinking of you. You'd like him."

"Paige, I'm perfectly happy with what I have."

"And that's what? A teacher old enough to be your father who hasn't made a move on you in four months. Come on Kori. You two wait any longer and you'll be looking at senior housing together."

Kori knew Paige wasn't fond of Elliot. Paige loved youth. She strived to maintain it in spite of having a birthday every year. When she turned thirty in May, she refused to recognize the day as her birthday. Paige was twenty-nine and she would stay that age for the rest of her life. For Kori to date someone older than thirty was beyond Paige's understanding. And it was made worse for Paige because Kori knew his age and continued to see him.

"I'm not getting into this discussion with you again. I'm happy where I'm at in life and I have no plans on changing anything."

"Except dead bodies turning up in your yard. Speaking of which, a Detective Bakker stopped by earlier."

"And?"

"And what?"

"What did he ask you Paige?"

"Oh just about Boyd and Elliot. What I thought of them. And he asked about Tyler. If I knew whatever happened to him. Stuff like that."

Kori wasn't sure if she should panic or not. The police asking about the men she had dated and one she'd married didn't worry her. The thought that Paige gave her opinion of them did. Kori decided to let it go. Asking Paige to expand would only frustrate Kori more. Paige would dance around her questions and then say something totally ridiculous and the conversation would end anyway.

"Well, I'm sure the police will catch him soon. With fingerprints, profilers, and DNA available to them, how long could this really take? Besides, some poor family has got to be getting worried about her." Horrible images came quickly to her mind and Kori shook her head as though the act would clear her memory. An uncomfortable silence fell between them until Paige finally broke it.

"Well, I'm tired. I think I'll just call it a night now. A mural on one wall Gabe and I scraped off just kicked my butt. And I definitely need a shower before Matt comes home. It's bad enough that you're seeing me like this but I shudder to think Matt would see this beautiful body so disgusting."

And off she went. There was no good-bye or a request for Kori to wait. Kori yelled up to her. "I'm heading home then. You're latte is on the kitchen table. I'll call you tomorrow."

"Thanks for the drink. Catch ya later." Kori was happy to be going home. It was getting darker out and she would only be too happy for her and Harley to get home before it was to dark to see clearly. And the smell of old glue was giving her a headache. Or maybe it was just Paige. She hated when Paige decided to fix her up with some guy. She always thought Kori would like them but she never really did. Of course, Paige used her own preference to what she liked in men to determine what Kori would like.

Harley had been a good boy. Last time at Paige's, he'd wandered around the house which set Paige off again. She didn't mind Harley as long as he kept any hair shed in one room. As they approached the front walk to her house, Harley stopped. "Come on boy." He didn't budge. Then he sat down. "What's wrong with you?" Kori looked at the house. Nothing seemed different. The front door was closed and all the windows were shut. The light in the foyer was on but that wasn't unusual.

Staring at the light, her heart rate accelerated. She didn't remember turning it on. They had left in the afternoon and she had been planning on coming back for the car. But maybe she had flipped the switch. She'd been preoccupied so it's possible she did it out of habit. Kori had deadbolts on both doors that required a key to get in or out. She left Harley and continued up the walk. In three steps she was at her door. If she turned the knob and it opened she'd run to a neighbor's and call Detective Bakker.

The door slid open with ease. But before she could turn and run a white envelope on the floor caught her attention. Her heart felt like it would beat right out of her chest and as she bent down to pick up the envelope she notice her hands were shaking uncontrollably. She knew in the back of her mind she might be damaging fingerprints but the envelope wasn't sealed. The flap had been tucked into itself. As she opened it she saw a picture with a note held onto it with a pink paperclip.

The picture was of the dead woman. But in the picture, she was still alive and well, sitting on a park bench with a book in her hand. The title was unreadable but it looked like a summer photo. The woman had on shorts and a sleeveless shirt and her blonde hair was held in a ponytail. Kori removed the note and saw one word on the back of the picture. Shelly.

Then she looked at the note. The same familiar half-inch block letters.

> Let Us play Yesterday
> I-the Girl at school-
> You-the Eternity-the
> Untold Tale

She reached the neighbor's door in less than a minute.

CHAPTER 2

After interviewing Kori Chandler, Detective Bakker walked back to the crime scene. His best friend, Detective Evan Harding was still down there. They had gone through the Academy together and both had made detective in the same year. Jonah knew people laughed sometimes when they were seen working a case together. They looked like Laurel and Hardy. Jonah stood six-two and weighed in at two hundred twenty pounds and though Evan was only two inches shorter, he only tipped the scale to 170.

And when faced with dealing with either Jonah or Evan, most criminals made the mistake of thinking Evan would be an easy target. They soon found that three-quarters of Evan's weight was muscle.

But they worked well together. On occasion, they would play good cop vs. bad cop in interrogations but mostly they complimented each other. They could see different sides of the same coin and because of that their solved cases outnumbered the unsolved. As Jonah reached the woods he could see the frown on Evan's face and that was not a good sign.

"Hey, Harding. Did you find anything?"

"No and you know that's not a good way to start. Whoever this guy is put some thought into this."

"Do you think we'll have much luck with the rope or knife? I'm not expecting prints but maybe we'll be able to trace it."

"Doubt we'll get that lucky. Looked like rope you can buy at any hardware store. Same thing will probably be true of the knife. I sent a couple of cops to start asking around town if anyone was seen walking in the development or in town past dark. It was cold so that might weed out night strollers. Did the Chandler woman offer anything?"

"The usual cast of suspects. Ex-boyfriend, new 'friend' she just started seeing, a girlfriend who knew she worked late, etc., etc. She says it was a mutual parting of the sea with the ex but I think I'll start with him and then work on the girlfriend, Paige McCleary."

"Who's the ex anyway?"

"Boyd Thomas. Is that special or what?"

Boyd had put in some time at Tabor College and being a frat boy made him and the police acquaintances. Now he was the manager of Keith's New and Used Car Lot. What amazed him the most is that Kori Chandler actually dated this idiot. Well, he wasn't an idiot just a con man and an opportunist. Boyd Thomas was the kind of guy that could convince you that your sins would send you to hell and he just so happened to have hand baskets on sale.

"Let's say we meet at seven at Tommy's. I should get to both by then and you can tell me what you've been thinking so hard about?"

"Sounds good to me. I'll tell you all my great theories. See ya later."

Jonah Bakker didn't like this a bit. A murder in a small town like Tabor was bad enough but when it got out about how the victim was 'displayed', all hell was going to break loose. He had been there when the crime technicians had done their job and he seriously doubted they'd get prints off anything. And he was almost sure the rope and knife would come back as common as a housefly.

Jonah liked to follow his gut instinct when possible. As long as he didn't come off as a moron he'd try anything to solve a case. What he couldn't understand was how the killer got the girl that far into the woods. He looked over the scene and even down the trail a bit and hadn't seen any drag marks. Though this didn't mean she went willingly he'd bet she did. Jonah would also put a stake in the idea she was a college student.

She and the killer must have met before at some time. Maybe he even knew her well. What really concerned him was that no personal effects were found with the body so what in hell happened to her clothes? If she was walking in the park she probably wouldn't be carrying a purse or keys but she would need clothes. And shoes would help immensely too. Did the killer take them for a souvenir? That scarred him the most. If he didn't burn or bury her clothes he most likely took them with him. And that was not good, not good at all.

Detective Bakker pulled into Keith's Car Lot. It was the typical lot with multi-colored pennants strung around the lot and every light on though the sun was out in full force. When he walked in and three salespersons stood up. The first to reach him was a round, plump little man with a ruddy complexion that came to Jonah's chin. He reached inside his jacket and showed him his badge.

"I'd like to talk to Boyd Thomas. Is he in?"

"Can I say who wants to talk to him Officer?" Smiling, he reminded Jonah of one of the munchkins in the Wizard of Oz.

"You can tell him Detective Jonah Bakker is here on official business. Thank you." Munchkin Man's smile faltered a bit but Jonah decided he recovered rather well.

When ten minutes had past, Jonah figured this was Boyd's little power play. Let the detective wait awhile since obviously the police were confused because Boyd hadn't done a thing. Jonah had already looked at every display model in the showroom and after another five minutes it was becoming almost impossible to contain his rising temper. Finally, he saw Boyd Thomas casually walk out from where the back offices must be located.

Considering his looks, Jonah could see why Kori had dated him. Boyd was good-looking by any woman's standards. He was about Jonah's height, give or take an inch, black hair that was slicked back and parted down the middle. What got the women was the slight waviness of it and eyes that could only be described as gray. He had what Jonah called the 'showman's smile'. That large, toothy smile that looked incredibly sincere though it only made Bakker think of a clown.

"Good morning Detective Bakker. I'm sorry to keep you waiting so long. Why don't we go back to my office so we can talk privately?"

Boyd stuck out his hand and shook Jonah's. His first impression was Boyd had probably practiced that shake. Not too lose or hard and probably made women feel safe in his hands. Boyd led him down a long corridor that had standard commercial grade carpeting in dark blue and walls painted a sky blue. Certificates and distinctions of employees were hung every foot or so till they reached Boyd's office.

His office was larger than Jonah had expected but that was about all that surprised him. Awards, distinctions, were strategically placed. Pictures with city council members and the Mayor were hung behind his desk so the first thing scarred customers would see would be the smiling faces of the people who ran their town. Jonah wasn't impressed with the show.

"Would you like a cup of coffee Detective?"

"No thank you. Just need to ask you a few questions."

"Should I call my lawyer?" Boyd gave his best clown smile.

"Not unless you think you need one."

"No Detective Bakker, I do not believe I'll need one. Just a little humor. Ask whatever you'd like."

"Let's start simple. Do you know Miss Kori Chandler?"

"Yes. We dated for quite some time and broke off the relationship about five months ago."

"Was it a mutual parting?"

"Yes. Like I said, we'd dated for a while. I wanted to get married, start a family and she didn't want any of it. We thought it best to go our separate ways instead of wasting anymore time going nowhere. Is Kori all right? Is she in some kind of trouble?"

"Last night someone murdered a young woman and then tied the body to a tree at the end of her property line. So you weren't pissed you spent two years with a woman who didn't want to marry you?"

"No, I wasn't pissed. We had a lot of great times together and I'm still very fond of her. She was married briefly; I think six months, to some guy in a band. They divorced and I guess it left her with a bad taste for marriage."

"Was she faithful in the relationship?"

"As far as I know she was. Kori's not the type to screw around."

"Know anybody who might be angry or upset with her?"

"I wouldn't know Detective. If we run into each other we hug exchange pleasantries but we no longer discuss our lives in depth. I have no idea what her life has been like since we split but when we were together I don't think I ever met someone that didn't like her."

"Well, that's it for now. Oh, Mr. Thomas? You do have an alibi for Saturday between eight at night and say three in the morning on Sunday right?"

"Yes, Detective Bakker I do. And if for some reason you need my alibi you can call my attorney for it."

"Thank you Mr. Thomas for you time."

"Anything to help Kori. Detective? If you want someone who knows Kori's life now you might want to check with Professor Elliot Bowman. I heard around town they're dating."

"Thanks." Asshole. Anything for the ex handing over her new love. What a jerk. But being an asshole and a jerk still doesn't make him a killer. He walked slowly through the showroom and out to his car. At least that unpleasant task was over for now.

He couldn't wait to see what Paige McCleary has to say.

Detective Evan Harding decided there were only two things that might be accomplished on a Sunday afternoon. After driving around town for a while then drove back to headquarters to make sure missing persons hadn't been reported anytime in the last week. None had come in matching his description of the dead woman. He found Sam Shawl sitting at his desk going over a few reports. Sam was good cop and had enough artistic talent to also be a part-time sketch artist for the department.

"Sam? Could I bother you for a few minutes?"

"Sure. What can I help you with?"

"Have you heard about the murder victim we got on Maple Lane?"

"Sure have. Press is going to have a field day with that. What about the murder?"

"I have an idea she may have been a college student. Think we could put together a quick sketch of her."

"I got about an hour to spare. Do you want to go into your office?"

An hour later they were done with the composite. Sam had done a very good job on it. He gave her a 'mug shot' appearance because neither one wanted to assume what her smile looked like. The hair was the right length and her features looked as Evan had depicted them but there was still coldness about the sketch. Evan guessed it was because they only knew her in death.

He had told Sam the woman was between twenty or twenty-five years of age but Evan thought closer to twenty was right. And the idea of a college girl was starting to feel right also. A woman missing even one night might be missed. A boyfriend would call and get worried if she didn't answer or her mother or friend would assume something horrible if she didn't show up to meet them somewhere. But college life was different. A woman living on campus could leave for a few days and not be missed until she didn't arrive for class.

Evan arrived at Tabor College about a half hour after Sam finished the sketch.

There was a small area with picnic benches not far from a dorm that housed women. He decided to camp out there for a little while and show the composite to women that passed by him. You never know when luck will cross your path. And Evan was hoping for a lot of luck.

In one hour he had to have shown the sketch to fifty girls and nobody recognized her. Obviously, Lady Luck was somewhere other than Tabor. He was tired of sitting around but the administration building was closed on weekends. And since he wasn't sure the dead woman even went here that ruled out calling the president's office until they got a positive I.D. on her.

He figured he might as well head back to the office for a while. He could start running background checks on a few of the characters they did have names for. Besides, it was already twenty minutes past three and he had to meet Jonah at six. That should give him enough time to do a quick rundown of Kori, Paige McCleary and of course, Boyd Thomas.

Jonah pulled up in front of what could be a gorgeous gray colonial home. The outside showed serious neglect over the years but the architectural beauty was still there. A wrap around porch surrounded the house though the roof sagged a bit and a few of the spindles from the railing were missing. The shutters were painted black and a few were apparently hanging by one screw. He walked up the four steps leading to the porch. Jonah could hear people laughing inside and had to wait a minute before his knock was answered. Paige McCleary was quite a beautiful woman. She had long, straight blondish brown hair that was tied in the back and pinned up in a bun. Her face could have graced any fashion catalogue. Her cheekbones were high and prominent, a narrow nose, full lips, square jaw and eyes that were such a dark shade of brown you had to look carefully to see were the iris ended and the pupil began. All that set on a body meant for a lingerie magazine.

At the moment though, this delicate creature was covered in paint. She was still standing in the doorway smiling when Jonah forgot he hadn't yet introduced himself.

"Afternoon. I'm looking for Paige McCleary." He prayed she was Paige and not a sister or some other relation or friend just visiting.

"I'm Paige. What do you need or are you selling something?"

"Detective Jonah Bakker." He pulled out his badge and she inspected it closely.

"I was wondering if I could take a minute of you time. It's about your friend Kori Chandler."

"Come on in. Excuse the mess though. I decided I couldn't live with a green living room one more night. Follow me, we can talk in the kitchen."

The kitchen was more of a disaster than the living room was. He had thought it impossible to have an uglier color than green until he saw the yellow kitchen. Then he noticed a man standing by the sink. He was tall with brown hair and wearing white painters coveralls. He was obviously washing out paintbrushes and turned when he heard them enter the kitchen.

"Detective Bakker this is Gabe Hathaway. He owns a small home improvement company. Gabe's been generous enough to help me paint the inside of the house along with the exterior eventually."

The two men shook hands. "I think I've seen you're van around town before. 'House by Hathaway' on the side, right?"

"That's me all right. Well, I'll just set these brushes in some water and you two can talk in private. Paige, I'll start on the trim heading up the stairs."

"Thanks Gabe. I'll be there in a while. So, Detective Bakker, what can I do for you?"

"Well, how well would you say you know Kori Chandler?"

"Like she was my own sister. I've known her for almost twenty years. We went to school together."

"Did you go to college with her?"

"No. I didn't go to college."

"Do you know her ex-husband?"

"Tyler? I know of him."

"Have any idea why they divorced?"

"Of course I do. He was in a band. Band members tend to have a lot of groupies. It takes a strong man to refrain from having sex with women who practically throw their half-naked bodies at you every time you play. Tyler wasn't a strong a man but unfortunately, Kori didn't figure that out till after the wedding. She left him and signed divorce papers a month later. In total I think they were married six months."

"Any idea where Tyler's at now?"

"No and I hope I never see him again."

"Are you aware of what's been happening with Miss Chandler?"

"If you're referring to the body in her yard, yes, I'm well aware."

"Do you think Tyler would be capable of this? Say as revenge for Kori leaving?"

"Tyler was into sex and music. The more the better as far as he was concerned on both accounts. I think the only thing that pissed him off about Kori leaving was he didn't have a woman waiting for him at home anymore. But unless this woman was killed accidentally during some kinky ruff sex; no, I don't think Tyler could murder someone on purpose."

"What do you think of Boyd Thomas?"

"I think Kori is rotten at picking men. He's arrogant, self-centered and egotistical. Self-serving comes to mind too. But no, I don't think he's capable of doing this either."

"And what about Professor Elliot Bowman?"

"Can't honestly say. I've met him a few times but I can't say I know him. I think he's too old for Kori but that's irrelevant."

"Do you know of anyone who's been upset with Kori lately or someone that may have held a grudge against her for a long time? Ex-employee, any other boyfriends?"

"Detective, Kori has owned the coffee shop for almost five years now. Of course there have been disgruntled employees but I can't recall anyone she ever worried about or that she mentioned had threatened her. And as far as I know, Tyler was the first guy she ever really dated seriously."

"So she was what nineteen when she was married?"

"Yes and she was twenty when she divorced."

"If she's owned the coffee shop since she was twenty-five, what did she do after she left her husband?"

"She worked in the bookstore with me. I am an only child and my parents were older when they had me. So on my twenty-first birthday my father signed over the store to me and he and my mother moved to Arizona. I made Kori the manager."

"Well thank you Miss McCleary for your time. If you think of anything else that may help us please give me a call."

She walked Jonah to the door and he said good-bye to Gabe who was busy painting the trim. The door closed behind him and he felt like he was no closer to the killer than he was at eight this morning. Maybe Evan has had better luck. Speaking of which, it was almost six and if he was going to get to Tommy's on time he'd better get a moving. Evan better have something to cheer him up.

Evan arrived shortly after six at Tommy's Bar and Grill. Jonah was sitting at the bar drinking a coffee. When Jonah saw him, he got up and met him halfway. "Let's get a table in the back." Evan knew the less Jonah talked the more he had on his mind. Jonah also hadn't smiled and though that worked well interrogating suspects he was usually an easy going guy that always had a smile for friends.

They got to their table and Jonah sat down heavily. Something wasn't going the way Jonah had planned. He had that pained look on his face when a case was starting to frustrate him.

"Jonah man, you gotta lighten up a bit. You're wrinkles are popping out and you look your age."

"I don't really give a shit about my age. What did you find out today?"

"Who do you want to start with?"

"Start with our favorite. Mister Boyd Thomas." Jonah propped his head up with both hands and clenched his jaw. Evan could see the muscles being constricted and loosened.

"Not much of a record. Four speeding tickets since he was eighteen and a DUI. Five years ago. Charges must never have been filed for whatever shit he pulled in college. He was born and raised here in Tabor, played baseball and soccer in high school, attended Tabor College and graduated in 1993 with a degree in Business Administration. One of three kids, his parents still live here, two sisters live in Newton Falls. Nothing really unusual about him. Unless you get a psychological profile, he seems normal. How'd the interview go?"

"About as well as the background went. I think he likes to be in charge if you take into consideration how long I waited for him. Likes to show off who he's done business with. Comes off as quite a jerk and I'll never understand why a woman like Kori Chandler would date him."

"Speaking of Miss Chandler, I found she was married. Some guy named Tyler Adams and it didn't last long. Next chance I get I'll run a check on Adams."

"Boyd mentioned the ex-husband. Did anything else come back on Kori?"

"Nope. Nothing on Paige McCleary either except she's married to a guy named Matthew."

"I don't know if I should be happy that nobody's coming back with a record saying they did a short stint in a mental ward or pissed because we're not getting anywhere."

"Jonah, you're starting to sound like me and that's not going to make the wife happy in the least bit. It's not as though we're at the end of our rope yet. By tomorrow we should have a name to go with the dead girl and I still have to check out Tyler Adams. I think I'll find out a little about Matthew McCleary too."

"Do me a favor. Check on a guy named Gabe Hathaway."

"How's he involved in all this?"

"Owns his own company. Fixes up houses, like painting, roofing, and repairs in general, I guess. Owns House By Hathaway and he's doing some work for the McCleary's. He was at Paige's house when she was expecting Kori this morning. Just covering all the bases."

Their food arrived and Jonah was starving. He managed two bites of his burger when his pager went off. He called the familiar number, listened for a minute, asked where she was and wrote the address on a napkin. Evan knew the dinner was over before Jonah said a word to him.

"Let's go partner. Miss Chandler has had a visitor and he left a small present for her too."

It took about ten minutes to get to Kori's neighbor's house. The Winkman's were both around seventy and at first, Jonah wasn't sure who looked worse, them or Kori. He figured this was the most action the Winkman's had seen in this neighborhood and were probably hoping if this didn't end maybe Kori would leave and take her problems with her. He took a seat across from Kori and examined the plastic bags that now contained the envelope and picture.

Evan went over to Kori's house with a couple patrolmen to have a look around.

Jonah sat staring at the evidence. He knew Kori had opened it but he doubted she compromised anything. The killer hadn't left any prints after a murder and Jonah didn't think he suddenly got stupid and left prints on paper.

"What time did you arrive at your house?"

"A little after 7:00p.m."

"Did you notice anything unusual before you reached the door?"

A patrol car was sent out to Kori's house the minute the call came in. The officer on the scene had briefly told Bakker what Kori told him. She was rambling about an unlocked door, the envelope, and something about a dog. Now Jonah just had to make sense of it all and sort it out as logically as possible.

"I had Harley, my dog, with me. He sat down before we hit the steps. I turned the knob and the door opened. I was going to run but saw the envelope on the floor and opened it."

"And the front door was locked when you left?"

"Yes. I locked it this morning after the police left and I used the back door to leave."

"You told the officer outside the lights were on in the house. Didn't you turn on any lights before you left?"

"No. I figured I'd be home before dark. I was supposed to stop and get my car but I wasn't going far so I just walked."

"Where were you coming from?"

"Paige McCleary's house."

"Miss Chandler did anyone know your whereabouts today?"

"I stopped by the coffee shop so Janine Crawler knew where I was headed. I spoke to Elliot Bowman and of course Paige knew I was coming."

"Do you have someone you can stay with tonight?"

"I can stay in my apartment above the coffee shop. Detective Bakker this guy is scaring the shit out of me but if I stay somewhere else isn't it going to look like he's winning?"

"Well, I can't say for sure what he's trying to do so it's hard to say if he's winning or not but I'd rather be safe than sorry."

"All right. He can win for the night but I'm coming back tomorrow if nothing else happens."

"That's fine. Just do me one other favor. Don't tell anyone where you're staying. Okay? I'll have an officer wait while you pack and give you a lift over there. Goodnight Miss Chandler."

"Goodnight. And thank you Detective."

Jonah found Evan standing by Kori's front door. Jonah told the young officer with Evan to wait for Kori to pack and drive her to the apartment. He also set up a car to sit out front of the store till morning.

The last thing he needed was another dead woman. But he had the uneasy feeling the games were just beginning for all of them.

"So did you find anything interesting Evan? Please tell me you found prints on the door, a wallet the guy dropped, something."

"I can tell you some things you're going to like about as much as I do. Wanna hear?"

"Not really but go ahead?"

"There were no prints on the doorknob, the doorjamb, or the light switch. None, zip, zero."

"Not a print from Kori Chandler either?"

"Nope. Everything must have been wiped. None of the neighbor's saw anyone, suspicious or not, close to the house. Did you notice anything special about the picture?"

"Polaroid. Taken during the summer or at least warm weather. Name 'Shelly' was written on the back bottom of the picture. Nice little poem was sent also. I'd like to bet we got a college girl in the morgue. And at least three people knew Kori wouldn't be home for a while."

"Who?"

"Elliot Bowman, Janine Crawler, and Paige McCleary."

Evan shook his head. "We got half a dozen people that know Chandler's habits on any given day, we got three or possibly more we don't know about that knew her whereabouts tonight. A picture that suggests this perp has been planning this for some time. We have squat on evidence, a dead girl, and no clue which one of our neighbor's might have killed the girl. And what in hell is up with these poems? What kind of nut is going to quote Emily Dickinson? Jesus."

They sat in the car tossing around ideas for a few minutes. He started driving back to Tommy's so Evan could get his car. "I think it's safe to say she's a college girl. Don't see why he's choosing that line about a schoolgirl if she wasn't. I'd also assume it's safe to say he's somewhat educated. You think it's dark enough nobody would notice a stranger messing with the front door?"

"No. But after talking to the neighbors, I wouldn't say this is a close knit community. They could all tell you who Kori was and what she looked like and that she owned Kori's Koffee downtown but that's about it. A few people mentioned her having a dog but nobody could remember his name. Personally, I wouldn't put my life in their hands. No one wants to get involved especially since it seems to be directed at Kori alone. Did she recognize the girl in the picture by chance?"

"Not really. Said she may have come into the coffee shop but not as regular."

"Do you really think knowing this dead girl's name is going to help us?"

"Maybe. Unless we have a real sick monster on our hands, she has to tie into this some way. And if we're right and the killer was stalking her since summer, she must have had some meaning for him. Just a matter of figuring it all out."

"If he gives us enough time before he hits again. Obviously he doesn't like to waste time."

They arrived at the parking lot for Tommy's. Jonah parked next to Evans car and watched him get out. "Evan? You think we missed something in Kori's background?"

"Like what? Are you still hoping for a stay at a mental ward?"

"No. I'm not sure. Just feels like something's there we're just not seeing."

"Jonah, I went over her records. Unless I missed another husband nothing stood out."

"Maybe there's another boyfriend we're missing."

"Guess you'd have to ask Kori about that."

"Or Paige," Bakker added.

"Or stick to the current boyfriend."

"Elliot Bowman. Ever have reason to run into him?"

"Nope. Just know he teaches at Tabor College."

"Does it strike you as odd that this dead girl probably went to Tabor?"

"A little. What might be odd is the fact that Professor Bowman teaches English. That still covers poetry these days doesn't it?"

"I don't know but come tomorrow morning I will."

"I'll meet you at the cafe. I think I'm going to have a talk with Janine Crawler."

Kori packed as little as she could. She was scared but killer or not she refused to be chased out of her own home. The officer waited for her and then drove her to the apartment. He went in first and checked out every room and then they both went downstairs. Again he searched the rooms and she made sure the security system was on and working. The officer left but he didn't go far. Kori noticed the unmarked car sitting outside the cafe. She wasn't sure if she felt safe he was there or worried that Detective Bakker thought she needed to be watched.

Kori stood staring at her phone. She had promised Detective Bakker she wouldn't tell anyone were she was tonight but the local news had picked up the story and mentioned the dead woman on the six o'clock news. She was certain the news would have it again at ten and that worried her. Her mother always watched the late news and Kori didn't want her hearing about this mess from a newscaster. She should also let Paige and Elliot know that she was okay even if she didn't tell them where she was. Paige would be curious, but Elliot would worry and she didn't want him to worry. Kori sat down and started dialing her mother's number.

He knew she would come here. He watched as she and the police went in and lights came on upstairs and then down. The police officer came out and sat in the car and thought he was actually protecting her. He laughed at the ridiculous thought. He could be inside in less than a minute but people always underestimated him. They should know by now he had "special" talents and abilities but somehow they were overlooked. Sometimes it frustrated him but most of the time he remembered those that thought they were better than him were really just jealous.

Kori wouldn't be jealous of him. She would be able to see him for all his glory. A little bit longer and she would understand. He watched her through the window. She paced when she talked on the phone. She liked to play with her hair too. He could almost see the day he would run his fingers through her hair and feel the texture of it, be able to smell the fragrance of her shampoo.

He was getting to her. He could see the lines of stress on her forehead. Kori would eventually know the power he held in his hands. He would do anything for her, even kill. Most men weren't like that. And woman today had the right idea. They wanted men who were strong and manly yet sensitive and in touch with their feelings. Not only was he all that but he could also express his inner feelings with the perfect gift to the woman he loved.

Though women had the right idea about men, they were still a problem. A simple "thank you" was all he ever got and sometimes a smile. If only they knew the extent of his feelings. Then he met Kori and it felt like every nerve in his body was standing on end. He felt in tune with her. A oneness with her that he had only once felt before and knew he would never feel it again for anyone but Kori. And he believed she felt the bond between them too. She just hadn't realized that she was special and that there was a man truly worthy of her.

He had searched for awhile for his mate. Kori came to him in the most unlikely way. He had decided it was fate. He had almost thought he'd never find the woman who could appreciate his endless love. In the beginning, he thought he'd found his special woman but it hadn't worked out. He almost believed he'd never find another. But now fate was on his side and he knew he wasn't alone in the world. He had become less obtuse in his beliefs. Kori was special. He knew that the minute he met her. It was a knowledge that came from deep within his soul. He had to have her. She only needed a little persuasion and a push in the right direction.

The problem he was having though was that she seemed not to understand what he would go through for her. Didn't she realize the trouble it took to find a girl worthy enough to die for her? Perfect enough to give as a sacrifice of his love? Obviously Kori wasn't on the same wavelength as he was. So far, all she had done is drag the police in and run from her house.

He never saw the police as a problem though. They always thought they could figure him out by analyzing and stereotyping him into some kind of monster. They were slow learners. He was good at what he did and he was always careful. They wouldn't catch him unless he wanted them too and he was too busy to amuse the police by letting them get him. He worked far too long to be at this moment in time. It was the perfect time and place. And the prize of a lifetime awaited him in the end.

He continued to watch Kori on the phone. The bumbling idiots that called themselves police sat idly in their car. Not more than fifteen yards away and they didn't even know it. He wondered who she'd called first. Probably Paige but soon her first call for safety and security would be to him. He would deal with Paige later. Kori might be frightened for a while but that was okay. The intensity of his love and the power within him could be frightening but soon Kori would understand.

The thought of another "special" person loving him and understanding him was enthralling. A life with Kori. That single thought is what kept him going. She moved across the living room and stood in front of the windows. For a moment he thought he connected with her. Her unknowing eyes had met his and the moment sent a shiver down his spine. She was so beautiful. He could sit and watch her all night but he had things to do. Soon she would be his. Soon.

CHAPTER 3

Gabe Hathaway wasn't quite sure if he liked working for Paige McCleary or not.

She could be the sweetest person one-minute and complete bitch the next. Moody didn't begin to describe Paige. She was the most self-centered woman he'd ever met and couldn't image what kind of man married her. He had yet to meet her husband Matt. All he really knew was that the man might have trouble telling the difference between a hammer and a wrench.

Gabe ran five miles every morning. He liked to get up at six in the morning to ensure plenty of time to run, get home and shower and be at the job by eight. This morning, like the rest of the week, he had plenty of time. When he took the McCleary job, Paige adamantly stated he was not to arrive before ten a.m. She wanted her husband to be off to work and time for herself before she had a contractor under foot. He had no idea she planned to help him.

The inside of the house was actually better than the outside. It was an old house but solidly built. It was mostly cosmetic work that needed done. Paige dove into the painting with more enthusiasm than he expected. And she wasn't all that bad at it either.

As long as he caught her in the right mood, she was a good worker. Even her bad moods, she was still nice to look at.

He finished putting his running shoes on and headed out the door. Gabe moved to Tabor about eight months ago. He bought a condo in the "new" development and poured what other money he had into starting his business. The company was doing well enough that he was thinking about hiring on a helper. He ran through the paved parkway around the lake and headed for downtown. He liked the feel of Tabor though nothing compared to Cleveland with its tall buildings and wide streets.

He hit downtown and could see the sign for Paige's bookstore. She had told him that it started with her father and on her twenty-first birthday he'd signed over the place to her. Must be nice to inherit a good business. At twenty-seven, Gabe decided he'd done all right for himself. His parents had died when he was sixteen. His father owned half of a contracting business building homes. His Uncle Keith owned the other half.

Keith was actually his mother's brother but that didn't stop Gabe's father from going in half on a business with him. Keith had taken him in after his parent's death. When Gabe was eighteen he was given his father's share of the business and it went well enough for a few years. Then he decided it was time to spread his wings and sold out to his uncle.

He traveled for a while but finally decided to settle in Tabor, at least for a bit. He past Kori's Koffee and noticed the light on above the shop. She must have high tailed it out of her house after the body was found. The body was front-page news in Tabor. He planned on reading the whole article when he got back home. Gabe had stopped in the cafe before but had never met Kori there. He was usually a morning person so he was familiar with Janine.

He continued to jog his way home but thought maybe he'd stop in before Paige's house and buy her a coffee. He'd probably screw that up though. Gabe had a feeling she went for something more complex from a coffee shop. Well, if anyone knew what she drank, Janine or Kori would.

Gabe pulled in to the parking spot in front of Kori's Koffee at eight fifteen. An unmarked police car was parked in front of him. He wondered if he should go in or not but the "open" sign was on so he went in. He'd seen a picture of Kori at Paige's house so he knew it was Kori behind the bar this morning. Seated all the way in the back was Janine and who he guessed was a cop.

Kori smiled at him as he approached the bar. She looked just as beautiful in person as she did in the picture he'd see. She looked a bit tired but he guessed that was to be expected. He smiled at her.

"I don't think I've ever seen you here this early."

"I usually leave mornings to Janine but she's busy right now. Can

I get you something?"

"Just a regular coffee." He handed her his travel mug and had a seat on one of the stools at the bar.

"Is that it?"

"Well, that depends. I'm working on Paige McCleary's house. Any idea what she likes to drink?"

"As a matter of fact, I do. A caramel latte with two shots of espresso. But I also know that if you show up before ten during the week she's likely to tear your head off."

"I figure if I come bearing gifts she might let me live and I could get a jump-start on the day."

Kori laughed. The only thing that might save him is the fact that he really is good looking. It really didn't matter too much if he came with espresso or not. Paige really liked things done her way and on her time. "I guess you must be Gabe."

"Yep." He smiled again. Kori liked his smile. It came easily and made his whole face light up.

"Well, try and have a good morning with Paige."

"I'm sure I will. Bye Kori."

"Bye."

Detective Harding sat in the back corner of the coffee shop with Janine Crawler. They'd been there for about a half an hour and he could tell she really didn't know anybody that would want to stalk or kill Kori Chandler.

"So there's absolutely nobody you can think of that may be capable of this?"

"I told you Detective; Kori's not like that. I think I've seen her fire two people in the three years I've been here. And those two called off all the time and showed up late if they even bothered to come in. They were useless and even they knew it. She doesn't date every guy that walks in here. And as far as I know, she doesn't tend to piss people off for no apparent reason."

Evan could tell she was getting exasperated. He was on the verge of it also. He was getting nowhere. Just then a guy walked in and the look on Janine's face said it all. She knew him and then Evan heard Kori say the name "Gabe".

"Who's that guy?"

"The guy that just walked in? That's Gabe Hathaway."

"Of 'House by Hathaway'?"

"Yep, that's him."

"Does he come in often?"

"Maybe twice a week. Mostly mornings though I've seen him here once or twice in the morning or mid-afternoon."

"Do you know him well?"

"No not really. Usually just gets coffee and goes. We talk pleasantries while I get his coffee."

"Okay. I'm going to give you my card. If you think of something or see anything that strikes you as different or out of the ordinary just give me a call. Thanks for your time."

Harding went to the bar and sat down. He used to come in quite often in the evenings but hadn't lately. But his first impression of Kori was still accurate. She was a 'people person'. The job fit her and he had a hard time seeing her doing anything else. He smiled and asked if he could get another cup of coffee.

"Thanks for letting me steal Janine."

"No problem. Anything to catch whoever did this. Any word on who "Shelly" is?

"Not yet but we're expecting a call soon. Do you work mornings often?"

"Only if I can't help it. When I first opened this place I was here from open to close. I lived upstairs for the first three years. Once I hired Janine and got her trained she said she'd be okay with opening herself. Now I mostly work in the afternoon and evenings."

"Janine mentioned seeing that guy that was just here a couple of times. You ever see him before?"

"Can't say for sure. He looks familiar though. I know his name is Gabe Hathaway. He's doing some painting for my friend Paige McCleary. But the only times Janine and I really work together is on Thursday's for Poetry Night and sometimes on Saturday's for the local bands we get in but it's usually nuts in here."

"Janine looked like she might have a little crush going on for him."

"She's twenty-five. Any guy that's cute and in the same age range is fair game for her."

"Does she date a lot of guys that come in here?"

"I honestly wouldn't know. We're friends but we keep it on a professional level. She might tell me how a date went but nothing detailed and vise versa. I need to start inventory now. Is there anything else I can get you before I go?"

"No thank you. I'll just wait here for Bakker."

With that Kori walked into the back room. She didn't particularly like Detective Harding. At least not as much as Bakker. She felt like he was trying to tie Janine into all this and that was just stupid. Janine and her really had nothing to do with each other outside of work. Plus, she had four other employees. Why didn't they want to grill them?

She was getting more pissed off by the minute. How absolutely stupid could they be to think Janine knew anything? And now Harding is sitting at the bar waiting for Detective Bakker. Maybe she should get rid of the bagels and order in some donuts. Why the hell not. The dead girl not only made the television news but also the paper so why wouldn't the police be camped out at her store?

Kori would also like to know just where exactly Detective Bakker was. What other friend of hers was getting harassed at nine o'clock in the morning. She stopped herself there. She felt horribly guilty all of the sudden. Here she was getting ticked because her life was a little messy right now and that poor girl was dead and God only knew what her family was going through.

She noticed then that Bakker had just walked in. She wished she were able to read the expression on his face. Was he tense? Did he know who 'Shelly' was? Well, she'd know soon enough. If they had something she was sure they'd tell her.

Gabe decided Kori was right. Paige had the temperament to tear into him if he showed up too much before ten. No sense in getting her in the bitch mode right off the bat. Kori had made the latte extra hot just in case he opted to drive around for an hour and save himself. After the coffee shop he drove to the hardware store. He was tempted to drive to Newton Falls to get to the retail chain but wasn't in the mood for that.

He killed enough time so that he arrived at Paige's house at nine-thirty. Maybe he'd keep his head intact for only being thirty minutes early. He parked in the drive and went around to the back door. Paige opened it wearing what Gabe could only describe as "skimpy" for a cool September morning.

"You're early." That was it. She left the door open and walked away. He guessed it was safe to enter. She really wasn't a morning person.

"Yeah, sorry. I stopped by Kori's to get coffee. I brought you a latte. Kori said you like this kind."

"Huh." She took the cup, sat down at the table and went back to reading the paper. Not even a 'thank you'. Gabe was getting real tired of the bitch mode and he'd only been there for five minutes. He desperately wanted to lay into her but there were things to be considered.

First problem was, she was his paycheck. He just gave another quote on a house the other day but so far this was it. He hoped this would take him into October and have another job lined up in another week or so to start after this.

Second problem was, he had a hard time yelling at such a gorgeous woman. Paige was one of the fortunate women that looked great even without make-up and her hair a mess. Not to mention the pajama's she slept in. It looked like such a lightweight of cotton she could wear it during a heat wave in July and not break a sweat.

He'd found himself staring at her a few times in the past week. Once it got so bad he had to imagine what his aunt would look like naked in the morning just to get control of himself. She continued to sit at the table and blatantly ignore him.

He took off his jacket and sat down across from her. He had to

say something before he felt like a complete ass.
"So where you want me to start today?"
"Doesn't matter. Wherever you want to is fine."
Now this was a change. Even in her worst mood she liked to give him orders. He sat for a minute trying to figure out what her problem was. Was she really that pissed he showed up a half-hour early? But if that was it why didn't she just tell him to go back out and come back at ten? He was about to expand on this line of thought but figured it would just waste brain cells trying to sort out what motivates Paige McCleary.
"In that case, I think I'll finish the stairway and work toward the bedroom. Since the murals off we might as well get that room done. Unless your husbands still home."
"He's gone. "
"Well, I'll get started then."

It took an hour before he had trimmed the wall by the steps, rolled the first coat on the wall and started the second coat of trim. Paige spent that hour in the living room arranging furniture and deciding where pictures were going to be hung. She hadn't said a word the entire hour.
After he finished the trim and rolled the second coat he took the paint and brushes to the kitchen and started cleaning. Paige had chosen to go with an ivory for the upstairs hall and her bedroom so when he finished cleaning he grabbed the paint and headed upstairs. Paige was still picking her way around the living room.
Gabe loved the bedroom. The first day he was there, they'd decided to knock out a wall between the master bedroom and main bathroom so there would be a private master bath. There was another small bedroom on the other side of the bathroom they would get rid of and make another bath and a storage area with the other half of the room.
Gabe suggested they knock out the wall and put in the doorframe and deal with the bathroom later. At least the bedroom would be back to normal. The only problem Gabe had was that Paige said the

king-size box spring and mattress would have to stay in the room. Matt didn't care if the frame of the bed was gone but he insisted the rest of the bed stayed. Gabe was told he would just have to work around it.

He hated working around obstacles. A king size mattress was definitely an obstacle for him. No use complaining about it so he got a huge plastic drop cloth and covered it. The woodwork would stay its natural color so at least he didn't have to worry about painting doorframes and baseboards. He'd just opened the can of paint when he heard footsteps approaching. Well, maybe he was going to get lucky and the princess was going to talk to him today.

Gabe knew she was standing in the doorway but he continued to trim out the closet door. A good five minutes passed and all she did was stand and watch him. He started to get irritated but figured if she wanted to watch instead of help that was fine by him. He usually worked alone anyway, he was just getting spoiled with her helping. Finally, she spoke to him.

"Gabe? Can I ask you something?"

"Sure. Shoot."

"Do you think I'm attractive?"

For a second, he thought he'd misunderstood her. "What?"

"I asked if you thought I was attractive?"

"Is this a trick question?"

"No. Simple question. A simple answer will do fine."

"Yes. You're an attractive woman."

"Attractive in general or specifically attractive to you?"

"Both."

"Do you find me sexy also?" She had closed the distance between them to mere inches. He could feel her breath on him, feel the heat from her body. He was going to get into trouble. He could feel it.

"Yes."

That was what she had been waiting for. The second his answer was out her mouth closed on his. It was a slow, sensual kiss that left no room for question what she wanted. She pulled away and led him to the bed. Paige turned long enough to rip the drop cloth off and turned back to Gabe. She took his hands and put them under her shirt pressing them against her flat, bare stomach. Slowly sliding his hands up until he cupped his hands around her breasts.

He gently caressed her breasts until he felt her nipples harden under his touch. She let out a soft moan of pleasure and moved her body an inch closer to his. She unbuttoned his jeans and slid her warm hand down his pants.

She whispered in his ear. "Am I responsible for this condition you're in?"

It took him a second but finely he got out a yes. She continued to stroke him and softly breathe in his ear.

"If I've done this to you, I feel obligated to provide relief. So what'd ya say Gabe? You wanna fuck me or not?"

"Absolutely."

They made love again and an hour and a half later they were still lying in her bed. Gabe knew he was about to ruin the moment but he couldn't stand it anymore.

"Paige?"

"What?"

"Where's your husband?"

"Probably fucking somebody else."

"Should I ask how you know this?"

"No."

He wasn't sure what else to say. This definitely was a first for him. He'd been with a few women but none had ever been married. At least as far as he knew they weren't. Well, he wasn't going to worry about it now. Sometimes you just had to run with what fate gave you and fate had given him the best lay he'd ever had. He wasn't going to end this.

"Gabe? I know men talk sometimes but you breath a word about this and..."

"I'm not going to say anything"

"Thank you."

"You have any idea when Matt's going to be home?"

"Late I suppose. Well, this was fun but we do have work to do." She got up and left. Five minutes later she was dressed for painting and so was he. They painted for a couple of hours and then took a break for lunch. They went back to painting and by four o'clock they had finished the bedroom and hallway.

There were two small bedrooms across the hall from Paige's bedroom. She had bought a light peach paint for one and soft yellow color for the other. After they ate pizza for dinner, she started painting one room while Gabe started the other.

Gabe was completely amazed by the fact that Paige had not even mentioned them having sex earlier. She went on with the day as though nothing had happened and he wondered if that meant it would never happen again. He guessed it really didn't matter. He'd like to be with her again but if that didn't happen it wouldn't kill him.

He left her house around seven that night. She kissed him goodbye and thanked him then turned and closed the door. He almost thought this was going to rank up there as one of his best days until he got to his driveway. That's when he noticed the same unmarked police car he'd seen this morning at Kori's parked there. As he pulled in a detective stepped out of the car

"Are you Gabe Hathaway?"

"Yep. What can I do for you?"

"I'm Detective Evan Harding. I was wondering if I could have a minute of your time?"

"What's it about?"

"Kori Chandler."

"Sure. Come on in Detective."

Gabe led Detective Harding through the living room and into the small kitchen: "I'm not sure how much I can help you Detective. I've only really met Kori Chandler once."

"Well, we just like to cover all the bases you know. Janine mentioned you came into Kori's Koffee occasionally."

"Yep. Couple times a week at least. Sometimes I'd go there on poetry nights or if there was a band I'd heard of playing on a Saturday

I'd go."

"Have you ever seen this girl before?" Evan showed him a picture of the dead girl. The girls I.D. came back earlier that morning. Her name was Michelle Roberts but everyone called her Shelly. She was a sophomore at Tabor College. Her roommate said occasionally, Shelly would stop in the morning and get a coffee or grab a hot chocolate and go study in the park in the late afternoon.

Gabe looked at the picture for few seconds. "I can't say one way or another. She looks familiar but, not to sound mean, some of those college girls look a lot alike."

"I know what you mean. Her roommate also said she would go to the poetry readings at the coffee shop."

"I've only gone a few times. Something to do on a boring Thursday."

"How long have you lived in Tabor?"

"About eight months. Moved down from Cleveland."

"You like it better here?"

"Yeah. For the most part. I don't have many friends here like I did there. Been busy setting up the business. Not much time for socializing."

"I guess not. No family around here?"

"No. My parents died when I was sixteen and I'm an only child."

"That must have been rough. Get sent into the system?"

"No. I had an aunt and uncle that took me in. It worked out."

"That's good. Well, thanks for your time."

"Hey, no problem.

At the same time Detective Harding was talking to Gabe, Paige was having her own set of problems. It was eight o'clock and Matt was just pulling in the drive. He walked in the kitchen and threw his briefcase and jacket on the table. He walked over and gave Paige a kiss on the cheek. She had turned her head so he had no other option but her cheek.

"So how was your day? Get anything finished?"

"The day was fine. Finished a few things."

"Something the matter Paige?"
"Where've you been Matt?"
"Work. A client of ours is being audited so we need to go over the books again. Why?"
"Where were you last night?"
"Paige, I've been working. This is our biggest client that's in deep shit. Why the inquisition?"
For a while she considered not even saying a word. She'd let whatever he was doing slide by but she just couldn't bury her head in the sand. If it had been work she would have tried to be understanding but she knew it wasn't. Well, at least work wasn't the whole picture.
"So you went to your mother's house Sunday morning and then what? Decided to go to the office to work till ten? Isn't that what time you finally got home?"
"Yes I went to my mother's. She's not feeling well. I called here around seven but you didn't answer and the machine isn't hooked up yet. If you would have answered I would have told you I was going to the office for a while. I figured you'd be painting."
"Ah. I see. It's my fault now because I didn't answer the phone."
"Paige what in hell is your problem?"
"Didn't you call your mother before you left Sunday?"
"Yes. So? You have a problem with that too?"
"Well, you see, I didn't have a problem until I decided to be brave and call her house to find out what time you planned on coming home. And you know what happened don't you, Matt? Since when did your mother have her phone turned off?"
He stood and stared at her. He didn't move, he didn't offer an explanation, he didn't utter a single syllable. What she did see though was the change in his eyes. Where she once saw love there was something else. Paige felt like her heart was being ripped out. She wanted him to tell her it was all a mistake. She wanted him to say she was wrong, say anything because all she saw staring back at her was indifference.

CHAPTER 4

On Tuesday morning Elliot Bowman arrived at the office at seven o'clock. He normally didn't go in till eight but he had given a writing assignment last week and had yet to get the grades into his computer. He was about half way through the grades when he heard a knock on his door. He turned and finally met Detective Bakker.

"Professor Bowman, I'm Detective Bakker. I was wondering if I could have a minute of your time?"

"Sure. Have a seat Detective. I suppose this is about Kori."

"Indirectly, yes. More to the point, it's about a student of yours."

"Which one?"

"The girl that was killed Saturday night was Michelle Roberts. Do you know her Professor?"

"The name is familiar but I teach two freshman English classes and two classes of American Literature. I have over a hundred and twenty students and it's the beginning of the year."

"So you don't know her by name?"

"No. Do you have a picture?"

"As a matter of fact I do." Jonah pulled out Shelly's college I.D. Elliot looked at it closely and realized he did know the face if not the name.

"Yes, I've seen her before. I have roughly thirty students in my two o'clock American Lit class. The class meets on Monday, Wednesday, and Friday. I think I spoke to her on Wednesday or Friday."

"Do you remember what you talked about?"

"Not really. I think it had something to do with the book I assigned."

"Which book is that Professor?"

"*The Sound and the Fury* by William Faulkner."

"Do you ever study poetry in this class?"

"Not really. If the author we are on has written poetry along with novels, we may touch on it but no, I don't necessarily focus on a poet."

"So you've never had reason to lecture about Emily Dickinson?"

"Not in my American Lit class. I've talked about her in my freshman English class when discussing poetry."

"Do you recall having Shelly in your freshman class?"

"I don't recall. I usually can remember if I've had a student before. I don't think I've ever had Miss Roberts in a class before."

"Did you ever see her at Kori's Koffee?"

"Not that I remember."

"Never on Poetry Night?"

"Not that I remember."

"Do you go in the coffee shop often for the poetry readings?"

"Maybe once a month unless one of my students is going to be there. Sometimes one will ask me to come if I can."

"How often do you go to the coffee shop?"

"In general? Three or four times a week."

"Aren't you dating Kori Chandler?"

"Yes."

"If she works nights and you're only there three or four times a week you must not see her a lot."

"Kori has a girl that closes the shop up at night. She's usually out of the cafe by nine except on Thursday's and Saturday's."

"You know her schedule pretty well Professor."

"Yes, it helps since I'm dating her."

"Is it an intimate relationship Professor Bowman?"

"And how would that information help in the investigation?"

"Just getting the feel of your relationship with Miss Chandler. Whoever is stalking her might not think too much of you and her if you are able to be with her and he is not. Telling me how intimate the two of you are also lets me know if this guy would see you as a threat."

Elliot considered what the detective was saying. He hadn't really given it much thought that the killer may not like Kori going out with him. He wasn't the kind of man to kiss and tell but in this case it might as well be known. "It is a nonphysical relationship."

"What exactly do you mean 'nonphysical'? Are you strictly friends or more but haven't had sex?"

"We have not been sexually intimate thus far."

"Was that a mutual agreement?"

"I don't know if we agreed on anything. Sex just hasn't played into the relationship yet."

"Have you ever seen a guy ask Kori out?"

"A couple of times. In the cafe."

"And she turned them down?"

"Yes."

"Did any of them get 'weird' about it? Seemed pissed for being rejected?"

"No, but then Kori can be very tactful in those situations."

"Does it upset you to hear other guys ask her out?"

"No. Kori is a very attractive woman. I think it would be odd if someone didn't ask her out."

"I see. Well that about does it for now. Thank you for giving me your time Professor Bowman. Here's my card. If you do happen to think of anything pertaining to Shelly Roberts please call."

"I will."

Elliot sat for some time after Detective Bakker left. He ran through the interview again and again and though the detective never said it, it sure sounded like he wanted to put Elliot at the top of the suspect list. He had a connection to the two major players in this game and that was never good even if he barely knew the one.

He tried for a while to remember Shelly Roberts but nothing jumped out at him. He talked to her but the conversation had been short. She'd asked something about the novel and something that could be found in the textbook. It just hadn't been all that important of a question to him. The kind that deserves a simple answer and really wouldn't generate a lengthy conversation. But still, he had talked to her.

And he really didn't like the questions the detective was asking about Kori and his relationship.

Whatever was between the two of them was private to him. It wasn't that he was hiding anything or trying to be possessive, he just liked to keep those things between Kori and himself. And it wasn't that he didn't want to sleep with Kori. She was an attractive woman and he did want her. He simply didn't want either of them to get hurt.

Kori didn't seem to have much luck with the men in her life and she showed a real distain for marriage. He was scared he'd lose her somehow and that would kill him. After his wife died he thought he would die along with her and, to some extent, a piece of him did. Elliot didn't have to think if he loved Kori, he knew that he did. But he feared if he told Kori that she'd feel pressured into loving him back and that would definitely scare her.

Besides, he knew she must be attracted to him or she wouldn't continue to see him but how much of her heart she wanted to invest remained a mystery to him. In all his contemplating though, he could see how odd this looked to an outsider. Two people dating for four months and neither one really knowing how the other felt.

Elliot completely lost track of time. It wasn't until a student in his English class knocked on the door to ask a quick question before class started that he realized the time. He'd wanted to call Kori and let her know Detective Bakker had stopped by but he didn't have time now. It would just have to wait.

Waiting to call Kori was probably the worst thing Elliot could have done all day. He'd completely forgot he had a departmental meeting at ten-thirty. After his class ended just before ten, he threw his stuff from class in his office and ran to make the meeting. By the time he called the cafe it was almost noon and Detective Bakker had already filled Kori in on the days events.

"Elliot, they make it sound like you're a suspect in all this."

"Well, Shelly Roberts was in one of my classes and we are dating."

"So what? I'm supposed to find it attractive that my boyfriend will kill a student and tie her to a tree for me? That is the dumbest thing I've ever heard! What do they suggest is your motive for all this?"

"I don't know. You'd have to ask them."

"That sounds like an idea. I'll have to remember that."

"Kori they're just doing they're job. I'm connected to both you and Michelle. I also teach an English class where I've talked about Emily Dickinson's poetry. The police almost have to look at me."

He could tell by the rise in her voice she was quite irritated. He could almost see her face getting flushed by anger. The detective was questioning all Kori's friends and she was protective of them.

"Why in God's name would someone I know want to do this to me? And I honestly don't think anyone I know would be capable of killing that girl. What that guy did to her was horrible. How could I not know if a friend of mine was really a monster that could do that?"

"Kori, could we have dinner tonight?"

"What?"

"Could we have dinner tonight? We're not going to get anywhere on the phone and I'd like to see you for longer than the twenty minutes you were in my office yesterday."

"Yeah. But I'd rather stay in."

"That's fine. How about I come over about six?"

"Okay."

"Be careful."

On a normal evening, Elliot would have knocked on Kori's door and walked in. Tonight he'd chosen to wait until she opened the door. He heard the soft, four-legged padding of Harley in the hall followed by Kori's footsteps.

"Hi. Why didn't you just come in?"

"I was afraid I might scare you."

"Don't be silly Elliot. This guy isn't going to knock on my door and waltz in here."

"He already did."

Kori stared at him, dumbfounded. He was right and they both

knew it. It scared him a little to think this guy did exactly what he usually did. Elliot wondered how long the guy has been watching her. Did he know she wasn't home or did he think she would assume it was Elliot?

"Elliot get in here. Is that dinner with you?"

"Yes. I hope you have a taste for Chinese. I brought Egg Rolls, Won Ton Soup, Moo Goo Gai Pan, and Beef Lo Mein. Hope you're hungry."

"I would say you're betting on it."

She laughed as they walked back to the kitchen. It had only been the day before that they found the body of Michelle Roberts but it seemed like ages since the last time he'd heard her laugh. If she had been wound earlier she seemed more relaxed now.

"How was the rest of your day?"

"Calm actually. I left the cafe not long after I talked to you. I thought Harley and I needed to bond a little bit. We came home and I did some laundry and cleaned up around here and then we played catch for a while in the yard."

"Sounds more fun than mine. Just classes and paperwork."

"Finish reading all the writing assignments?"

"Yep. And I finally got all the grades into the computer. Kori? Are you still planning to do Poetry Night this Thursday?"

"Yes. Why wouldn't I?"

"Well, for one thing the guy that's obviously taken with you is still a mystery unless you know something I don't. Second, he is writing you notes of poetry. Just wondering if Poetry Night might agitate this guy."

She put down her fork and studied Elliot for few seconds. He cared about her but he had never been obsessive or tried to tell her what to do. As far as she could remember he'd never even had an idea for the cafe that he'd told her about.

"Elliot, listen to me please. Yes, all of this scares me. I'm not even going to pretend that it doesn't. But I'm not going to let some sick, unknown monster run my life or my business. Every time I turn around I see the police, I've got Harley with me and I plan on talking to Paige and see if the guy that's helping fix her house can come and replace the locks on my doors. I won't live in complete fear Elliot. I can't."

She got up and took her plate to the sink. Whatever appetite she may have had was gone. She could feel the tears in her eyes. She'd never had reason to cry in front of Elliot and she didn't want to start now. Kori heard him get up and walk up behind her. He stood for a minute and then he wrapped his arms around her.

"Kori, I'm not trying to tell you how to live I'm just worried about you. When Detective Bakker talked to me today he asked me a lot about how often I was in the cafe. He also asked if I'd ever seen Michelle Roberts in the cafe. When I said I couldn't remember if I had or not he mentioned Poetry Night. And that worries me Kori. Since this guy is quoting Emily Dickinson, the police must be trying to tie this into the Thursday night reading or at least the cafe."

"Elliot the police have to look at the cafe. I spend more than half of my day there and occasionally I'm there all day. I interact with a lot of people. The cafe is a logical choice where this guy saw me in the first place."

"Is that supposed to make me feel better?"

"Elliot, I'll be fine."

"I'm counting on that."

She felt him hug her a little tighter. She wished it wasn't because some manic was playing a sick game with her that Elliot felt compelled to be so close to her. Kori liked the way it made her feel to have his arms around her. She had the idea to turn and slowly kiss him but he let go and the moment was gone as usual.

"So, how about building a fire tonight and just relaxing?"

"Sounds good. Why don't you build it and I'll clean up here."

Elliot left at ten and for the first time in her life, Kori understood the idea of pulling your hair out in frustration. Was he blind, unmoved by her, or just plain stupid? Could he really not see she wanted to at least kiss him with more passion than you used on your grandmother? Kori knew her only choice tonight was to call Paige. Paige didn't like Elliot but if anyone would know what to do it would be Paige.

The phone rang six times before Paige picked it up. Paige sounded so different for a minute Kori thought she might have woken her up.

"You sound odd, Paige. Did I wake you?"

"No."

"Something wrong?"

"Not really."

"Do you want to tell me?"

"No."

There was complete silence. Well, that was a first. Paige didn't tend to hesitate recalling an injustice done to her. Kori wasn't sure if she should press the matter or start rambling on with her problems. Maybe true confessions are what they both needed tonight.

"Feel like trying to solve my problems then?"

"Not really but go ahead."

"I wouldn't want to put you out or anything. Forget it."

"Kori is this a problem with Elliot?"

"Yeah, well, it's not a real 'problem'."

"Fuck him."

"Excuse me?"

"You heard me. Next time he's over just rip your clothes off and see what he does. If he doesn't throw you on the floor and do you right then and there he's married, gay, or not interested. And if any of those three apply, drop his ass and move on."

"Gee, thanks for the great advice. Remind me to ask for your opinion more often when you're in a shitty mood."

"Hey, you called me. I told you I didn't want to do this."

"What is your problem?"

"I also told you I don't want to talk about it right now. Is there anything else you need help with tonight?"

"Nope. I think I can manage the rest on my own."

"Fine. Good-bye."

Kori sat on the side of her bed with Harley at her feet. She went through the house twice checking that all the doors and windows were locked. Sitting there, she conceded this was the worst week in her life. If the pace kept up like this she'd be on sedatives by November.

In the past two days, she found a dead girl tied to her tree and the maniac responsible somehow got into her house to leave her a note. The police were asking questions about her ex-husband, interviewing her ex-boyfriend and her current one. Elliot was obviously missing every hint she wanted more from him and her best friend was just getting stranger by the minute.

Looking at Harley she said, "And what in hell is up with you? Huh?"

"First you hide behind me when we found Shelly then you refuse to go in the house when you apparently sensed someone had been in there. Am I supposed to be following your lead when you do these things? Do you think you could like bark if you hear something? You know I don't want to hear somebody breaking in and find you under the covers with me."

Harley just lay on the floor staring at her. "What are you looking at? You realize I'm the hand that feeds you? You are planning on protecting me aren't you? God, now I'm putting my life in your paws. And worse than that, I'm actually waiting for you to answer me."

"That's it. I'm starting to crack. I'm going to sleep. Good night buddy."

Wednesday morning came and went without much excitement so by Wednesday evening, Kori had hope for the rest of the week. She just wished the police would find the killer, Shelly could rest in peace, and if her friends would become halfway normal she could live her life contently. She hadn't heard from Paige and there was no way Kori was calling her until at least Friday. Paige has had her moments but this was by far her worst.

Kori did manage to track down the number for Gabe Hathaway and he'd called her Tuesday night. He said he could swing by around five tonight and that worked fine for her. Gabe seemed like a nice enough guy, and Paige was right about him being good-looking, but for the life of her she still couldn't understand why Paige thought she'd be interested in him.

So far the only thing that interested her was why he seemed so damn familiar. And the more she thought about it the more convinced she'd seen him before. It must have been at the cafe. It's not as though they traveled in the same circle of friends. Paige was their only connection. Oh well, no sense going crazy about it. She was almost sure they had met in the cafe before.

It was almost four o'clock and she knew she better get moving. She finished with the inventory list she was working on and found Janine at the counter. Something about Janine looked different to her but she couldn't quite put her finger on it. No, she wasn't going to go down that road. It was like she had a brain tumor or something that was making her see people in a new light. Well, whatever was going on with Janine she didn't want to know. Let sleeping dogs lie.

"Janine I'm going to head home now."

"Oh, okay. That guy's coming to change your locks today right?"

"Yep. He said five and I want to get home in time to shower. After playing in the stock room most of the day I feel like I have a thin coat of dust all over me."

"Have fun. I'll see you tomorrow."

If Gabe Hathaway was anything it was punctual. At five o'clock Kori saw a red truck pull in the drive. She got up and went to the door to let him in. As she watched him get out, she was again struck by a sense of familiarity. What was it about him? Who did he remind her of? Was it the way he walked? Before she could ponder it any longer he was at the door. Maybe she was going nuts.

"Hi. I'm Gabe Hathaway. We met at the cafe the other day."

"Hi. Yes I remember you. Thanks for coming out so soon Mr. Hathaway."

"Please just call me Gabe. And it's no problem getting out here. I'm not real busy right now. Paige's house is my biggest project."

"How's it going over there anyway?"

"Not bad. Upstairs is almost finished being painted."

"You guys are still painting? I thought that would be done by now?"

"We would have but Paige gave me today and yesterday off. Now you just have the front and back doors right?"

"Yeah those are the only ones that lead out."

"And you want to keep the same kind of locks? The dead bolts that you need to use a key to get in or out right?"

"Yep. Keeps me from locking myself out."

"Okay. I'll be done as soon as I can."

While Gabe worked on the doors, Kori kept busy with some paperwork she'd brought home. She liked to keep work at work but it didn't always happen. She'd found that when she had alot of paper to spread out her dinning room table was much easier than her office floor. It was about an hour later and she'd managed to get halfway through her printouts when Gabe walked in.

"Okay. You're all set."

"That didn't take long."

"It's not that hard to replace those sets. I also did a quick run through the house and made sure the latches on the windows were catching okay. Here are two keys. They open both doors."

"Great. I'll sleep better now. Thanks Gabe. How much do I owe you?

"I'm just charging you for the locks. I'll send you a bill."

"I have to pay you for your time."

"Don't worry about it. I've heard you've been through a lot lately. Glad I could help in some way."

"Gabe, please."

"Okay. How about having dinner with me tonight. We could go over to Tommy's and grab a burger?"

"I'm sorry I can't. I've really got to finish this paperwork."

"It'll still be here when you get back. I promise."

"I still can't Gabe. I'm sorry. I'm kind of seeing someone right now."

"It's only dinner Kori."

"I know but I don't think I'd like it much if he went to dinner with another woman even if she was just a friend."

"Okay. Hey, no problem. But if you starve tonight I'm going to remind you that you had your chance and passed on it."

Kori had to laugh. "I'll remember that." He had such an easy manner about himself. It surprised her a bit and he seemed quite comfortable with her saying no. She couldn't imagine he ran into that very often. Not too many women would turn down dinner with him she was sure. He grabbed his coat and toolbox and Kori followed him to the door. She stopped him as he headed out the door.

"Thanks again. And Gabe? I really am sorry about dinner."

"It's no problem. Don't give it another thought. Bye."

He smiled and she closed the door behind him. She took one of the keys and locked it right away before she forgot. She stood for a minute and watched him load his toolbox in the truck, get behind the wheel and pull out. Kori walked back to the dining room and saw Harley was still lying underneath the table. "Well, what do you say we get something to eat? Won't be Tommy's burgers but we can make do."

They walked into the kitchen together and as she got Harley's dinner ready he patiently watched. She would like to call Paige and find out why she gave Gabe two days off but then thought better. If she were still in her mood she wouldn't tell her anyway. Besides, Gabe could have asked for them off though she highly doubted it. If Paige were wearing the crown of Queen Bitch she wouldn't want anyone around.

Kori gave Harley his bowl and decided that on a cold night like tonight a bowl of clam chowder could rival a burger. And she didn't even have to go out for it. Maybe she should give Elliot a call and see what he was doing. She'd talked to him yesterday but hadn't heard from him today. She put the chowder in a bowl and threw it in the microwave. Kori dialed Elliot's number and listened to it ring and finally gave up.

"Obviously no ones in a hurry to answer phones this week."

She let Harley out the back and ate her soup. Afterwards she headed back to the mess in the dining room. By the time she finished it was nine-thirty. She thought about calling Elliot back but all she wanted to do was get into some warm sweats and curl up on the couch. Elliot would just have to wait till tomorrow. Hell, she's been waiting for months. Besides, she knew he'd show up for Poetry Night.

And Kori had the oddest feeling Thursday night was going to be quite interesting.

CHAPTER 5

Evan Harding decided there was no other place he'd rather be on a Thursday night than Kori's Koffee. When he told Jonah he'd like to meet there instead of Tommy's, Jonah agreed. Nodding, he said, "How's seven-thirty?"

"That's good for me."

Kori Chandler looked as excited to see them as she would be to see a couple of cockroaches. They could both understand that to a certain extent. Two detectives sitting in a coffee shop to hear poetry would seem a bit odd. And they were both sure Kori probably wasn't thrilled that Jonah had questioned Elliot Bowman.

The detectives chose a spot close to the door but with an excellent view of the stage. Evan went to the counter to grab a couple cups of coffee while Jonah settled in for what he hoped was a boring night. Since Kori was the target of the killer's notes, Evan and Jonah hoped he might show up for a little poetry. Evan returned with the coffee and they both took out their notebooks.

"How's Miss Chandler doing this evening?"

"I guess okay. Didn't look thrilled to see me. Or should I say us? Either way she doesn't look too happy about us being here."

"Well, she'll get used to it." Jonah let his gaze roll across the room.

"I think she'd rather we sat outside in the car."

"Can't hear what people are reading out there and you know how I love poetry."

"Don't roll your eyes, Jonah. Hey, maybe we'll take some culture home with us?"

"I don't give a shit about culture. I'd like to take home a killer."

"Speaking of which, look who just walked in."

"Think I should go and say 'hello' to Professor Bowman?"

"You do and Miss Chandler may just assault you herself."

They both smiled but refrained from laughing loudly. Elliot saw them as he walked in the door and sat down at the bar. He leaned over to say something to Kori and she glanced over at them with a look that was capable of turning them to stone.

"Okay Evan, with that look, you wanna bet he asked her if our presence would hurt business?"

"I like a bet here and there but I hate to lose too. I think I'll pass on that one."

"Did you ever locate Kori's ex-husband? What's his name? Tyler?"

"Not yet. Nothing since about ten years ago. Probably moved and/or changed his name."

They sat for the next forty-five minutes in relative quiet. They watched as people started to come in and find their spot for the night. Jonah figured most of them were regulars because Kori, Janine and another girl working knew a great many by name.

"Well, well. Look who just walked in the door." Evan set his cup down.

"What in hell is Boyd Thomas doing here?"

"Learning a little culture I guess."

"And isn't that his secretary on his arm?"

"Don't know about that. She's got nice legs though."

"You about ready for some more coffee?"

"You buying?"

"Yeah."

Jonah walked up to the bar. Must be interesting to have the new boyfriend and the old one in the same place. Boyd was still talking to Kori and neither they nor Elliot noticed him at first. If Janine hadn't asked if he needed anything he wondered how long he could have listened to their conversation. It seemed light and pleasant but then looks could be deceiving.

Everyone's attention turned to Jonah. Boyd was the first to speak.

"Detective Bakker right? Never expected you'd like poetry."

"I don't actually but I do like to keep people safe no matter where it takes me." He looked pointedly at Kori. "That is my job. Now, do you think I could get two more coffees please?"

Kori watched as he headed back to his table. She wasn't sure if she liked him here or not but she figured it couldn't really hurt. Maybe the monster will be bold enough to come in and throw himself at their mercy and beg for forgiveness. It was a long shot but hey, a woman can have her dreams.

Boyd had taken his leave and found a seat with his new woman. He hadn't introduced her, which was sort of rude, so she had no idea what to call her. And Kori still had no clue what would possess him to come here tonight. Elliot didn't particularly like him and he made it quite clear. He was almost moping at the bar.

"Elliot do you have a specific problem tonight or are you just pissed off in general?"

"Since you asked, yes I do have a specific problem. You're standing here."

"Well, I own this place so where exactly am I supposed to be Professor?"

"At home preferably."

Exasperated, she said, "And as I recall we've already had this conversation. About two days ago? This ringing any bells for you?"

"I know what you said but I don't have to be happy about it."

She shrugged. It was a losing battle. He was a walking contradiction. He gave her independence but he didn't want her working tonight. He cared but didn't want to sleep with her. He worried about her but he hadn't called to see how she was last night. If this kept up she was giving up on men and going to date Harley. She seemed to be able to handle her dog to some extent.

She made a couple of drinks and turned around to find Paige standing at the bar. Kori had planned on calling her tomorrow but that didn't seem necessary now. Before she could say a word Kori saw Gabe walk in. This was going to be an interesting night if nothing else. She glanced at Detective Bakker and knew not only his brain was going into over-drive but Detective Harding look as though Santa Claus just delivered the prized gift.

"I didn't expect to see you tonight Paige."

"I hadn't planned on it but figured what the hell."

"You can only stay if you're in a better mood. Rules of the house."

Paige looked at Elliot and frowned. "Really? So Grumpy over here, and Wyatt Earp and his sidekick in the corner can stay but I can't? Is that what you're saying?"

"I know why Grumpy's in his mood, and Wyatt's protecting the saloon and a damsel in distress. What's you're contribution to this evening?"

"Comic relief? I can be funny. Honestly."

Kori smiled. Paige had plopped down on a barstool next to Elliot and made herself comfortable. Gabe walked over and sat on the other side of Elliot. Obviously whatever was bothering Paige had passed or at least she covered it up tonight.

"Paige, you can stay. Elliot, have you met Gabe yet?"

"No." He turned and shook hands with Gabe. "Nice to meet you."

"Same here. Sleeping better with the new locks Kori?"

"Yep. Thanks again." She saw Janine over by the stage that was set up. "Janine? We almost ready to start?"

"Yeah. The first five people scheduled are here and ready. Might as well get going."

Kori dimmed the lights except for the set right above the stage. Elliot had told her two of the kids were students of his. The first girl was reading a passage by Robert Frost. She wondered if anyone would read something by Emily Dickinson. She prayed no one would because she had a feeling the detectives would be all over that person the minute they stepped off the stage.

Elliot looked as though he had the same thought. He seemed tense tonight and she couldn't believe it was all because of her. The news media was reporting notes found but not disclosing exactly what was in them. Kori figured that was the police department's way of sorting thru the nut cases that wanted the attention.

As Kori looked from the readers to Elliot and then to Gabe another thought crossed her mind. Maybe she should have been more specific with Gabe last night. She had simply told him that she was seeing 'someone' right now. Kori wondered if Gabe would mention his request for dinner last night and what, if anything, Elliot would say. Paige was oblivious to Kori's internal turmoil. Kori would like to reach over and slap her but Paige seemed to really be enjoying herself. And of course there was Wyatt Earp's reaction to worry about too.

At nine o'clock there was supposed to be a fifteen-minute break. Maybe after the break she should talk to Detective Bakker. Kori would really like to know what he and Detective Harding expected to discover here tonight. It irritated her to no end that they seemed to focus solely on her close friends.

There were only two more people waiting to read their original poetry after the break. Kori inched her way over to the table the detectives had occupied all evening.

"Could I talk to you for a minute Detective Bakker?"

"Sure. Have a seat. What's on your mind Miss Chandler?"

"What exactly do you hope to accomplish here tonight? What's the point of you two being here?" She watched as Bakker looked at Harding and back to her.

"To be honest, Miss Chandler, I'm not sure. I think this is where your 'admirer' first set eyes on you. It's known that some killers like to come back to the scene of the crime. Some like to immerse themselves in the investigation. I thought we should come and see some of the people that show up. Whether the killer is here or not I don't know."

"And it just so happens that some of my friends are in the same place that you're waiting to see if the killer comes to. Is that coincidence Detective?"

"Maybe. I don't know yet. You tell me. Are you sure you know all your friends well enough to say they aren't responsible?"

"Yes. I know I'm not 'friends' with a killer."

"So you're sure Mr. Thomas isn't secretly pissed you ended your relationship with him? Or that Professor Bowman isn't frustrated with how things are going with you? And do you know Mr. Hathaway well enough to make that call?"

"I've told you, Boyd and I made a mutual agreement to end the relationship. Elliot, to my knowledge, isn't frustrated about anything but me staying alone in my house and I wouldn't consider Gabe Hathaway a 'friend'. He's an acquaintance that did some work around the house."

"Could I ask you a question Miss Chandler?"

"What?"

"Do you know what happened to your ex-husband?"

"Tyler? No, I don't. I signed the divorce papers and never looked back. We didn't have anything to hold us together after that. There was no reason to keep in touch."

"So it wasn't a 'mutual agreement' when you divorced?"

Kori sighed and leaned back in her chair. "No, it wasn't 'mutual'. Tyler played the guitar and sang on some songs. He was very good and it always surprised me he never made it 'big'. But he got caught up in the moment and that usually landed him in bed with someone other than me. I got tired of it and left. I had my lawyer draw up the paperwork and I signed it. He met with Tyler's lawyer and eventually Tyler signed the papers. From what my lawyer said, Tyler didn't want the divorce."

"Why wouldn't he want the divorce?"

"He told my lawyer he still loved me and wanted to work it out. Whether he really did or not I can't say."

"Did he have any family?"

"His parents were dead by the time I met him. He had two younger brothers that I know of. I met one of them once after they played at a bar. I think his name was Jake but I can't be sure now."

"And you never met the other one?"

"No. I think the brother I did meet ran away and found Tyler that night at the bar. It wasn't what I'd call a joyous reunion. Tyler seemed peeved at the time. He never brought up the subject of his brothers and I assumed they didn't get along so I never pressed him on it."

"And he never mentioned any other family members?"

"No and I was too young and too in love to think it was strange. Tyler was kind of a loner. He liked the guys in the band and obviously he liked his women but he wasn't what you'd call a 'family man'.

Mind if I ask you why you're so interested in Tyler?"

It was Detective Harding that spoke up this time. "I ran a check on the name Tyler Adams and the information that came back was ten years old. Seemed a little odd."

"It would seem odd except when talking about Tyler. It wouldn't surprise me in the least if you found him leading a Bohemian life in the South of France with a rich widow."

"He sounds like a charming guy."

"I was young, in love and stupid. We're all entitled to a few mistakes aren't we?"

"Yes we are. And your mistakes are none of our business unless they've come back to haunt you."

On that note, Kori thanked both the detectives and excused herself. Bakker watched her go and then looked at Evan. Evan sat and drank his coffee. He had to know Jonah was staring at him but he refused to look at him.

"Okay Evan, I give. What the hell was that all about?"

"What'd ya mean?" Evan looked like he had the whole thing figured out and it was just about killing Jonah.

"I mean, why lead Kori to believe her ex is involved in all this or do you know something you're not sharing?"

"I've shared everything I know with you. Kori doesn't seem to believe anyone she knows could possibly want to hurt her. I wanted to plant the seed of doubt in her. If she can question a man she was married to then she can question men she's dated."

Jonah thought about it for a while before commenting. It was a good tactic that could pay off but, on the other hand, it could make things worse for Kori. "And what if she becomes so focused on her ex being a murderer that she runs right into the real killer's arms?"

"If she's with the killer then the notes and bodies should stop. We wait for a while and then put some pressure on whomever she runs to for support and comfort."

"Wouldn't Elliot Bowman be the logical choice here?"

"Maybe. But it doesn't sound like a real strong relationship right now. And right now she seems awfully comfortable talking to Mr. Thomas."

Jonah looked over at the bar. The readings had ended and people were gathering their things. Nobody looked out of place. Or weird enough to tie a girl to a tree. He wasn't exactly sure what he was looking for in a killer. Though if it was one of Kori's friends he came to the right place. A round up with a paddy wagon couldn't get the results he'd gotten tonight.

And Kori stood at the end of the bar chatting with Boyd Thomas. His woman was hanging back a bit and Jonah wondered if Boyd told her to backoff. Boyd and Kori seemed to be in a deep conversation meant for their ears alone. Jonah would like to ask Elliot how he felt about that but he stayed in his seat.

"Evan they were together for four years. That's longer than most marriages today. Hell, that's longer than Kori's marriage lasted. What I find more interesting is Paige McCleary sitting closely with Gabe Hathaway and seeming to be having a grand ole time talking with him."

"He's her house painter."

"Well, Elliot's sitting here and Paige and Gabe and even Boyd."

"And?"

"Where's Matt McCleary?"

Evan smiled. "I forgot about him. That's a damn good question. Should we go ask Mrs. McCleary?"

"Let's wait a second. This place is almost cleared out and Boyd should be leaving soon too. He doesn't have to know anything more than the media tells him."

They watched the last few customers leave and Boyd kissed Kori good-bye on her cheek. Janine was stacking chairs on the tables and Karen was starting to sweep. They both got up and put on their coats and headed to the bar. Paige turned and smiled at them.

"Detectives are you leaving so soon?" She gave them her best smile. Evan Harding returned her smile with his own.

"Well, we've had as much fun as we can take tonight. Maybe we'll stop back next Thursday. Will you be back Mrs. McCleary?"

Again he smiled.

"Oh, I might be. Guess you'll have to show up to find out."

"Will you be bringing Mr. McCleary next time?"

To everyone watching it was a little game they were playing. And to everyone watching Paige's smile was flawless but Evan didn't miss a thing. That beautiful smile faltered a bit and he caught it.

"Matt's not much on poetry. More into numbers than words. Sorry Detective."

Kori was watching and listening to this little tit-for-tat that Paige had going with Detective Harding. She was about to ask Paige what she was talking about. Matt had come with her several times to the poetry readings. Kori just opened her mouth when Karen walked up to the bar.

On Thursdays, Janine would wipe the tables off and stack the chairs on top and Karen would sweep and mop the floors. After that was done Kori usually sent them home. She didn't feel as rushed when she was cleaning up the bar and restocking everything if she was on her own. She'd seen Karen take the broom out to sweep but got caught up in the conversation to really notice what Karen was doing.

"Kori? Sorry to interrupt but I found this on the floor."

"Thanks Karen."

Karen had handed her a small white envelope. Kori absently started to open it while she turned her attention back to Paige and Detective Harding. She pulled out a napkin from the coffee shop and looked at it. Strange was the first word that popped into her head until she turned it over. In small block letters was a poem.

All her blood must have been pulled to her heart to get it to pump as fast as it was. Detective Bakker turned to look at her about the same time.

"Jesus Kori. You're white as a ghost. You feel all right?"

"Karen found an envelope. This was in it." Kori handed him the napkin. Her voice sounded weak and distant to her own ears. She wondered if this was what happened before you passed out or maybe she was going into shock. She sat down hard on the chair behind the counter. Kori could see Bakker's face turning red and hear him yelling. What was he saying? Something about locking the doors? She couldn't focus enough to understand him. Elliot was behind her then and that's the last thing she could remember.

She was only out five minutes but a lot happened in that time. Detective Bakker had the doors locked and police dispatched to the coffee shop. Detective Harding escorted Paige, Gabe, Janine and Karen upstairs to her office. Elliot demanded to stay with her and Bakker finally agreed. When the police arrived, Harding was taking the group upstairs into another room to question them separately.

Detective Bakker was sitting at a table with Elliot and Kori. Elliot must have carried her over because she woke up sitting in a chair leaning up against Elliot.

"Kori I'm sorry we have to do this now but I need to ask you some questions and it can't wait."

"I'm okay. I think it just shocked me to know I must have been in the same room with him all this time."

"Kori, I need you to look at this note again. Do you recognize the handwriting?"

"No. Not off hand."

"Do you recognize the poem?"

"No."

"You've never seen this poem before?"

Kori looked at it again and reread the poem.

Good to hide, and hear'em hunt!
Better, to be found,
If one care to, that is,
The Fox fits the Hound-

"I've never seen this before or heard it nor does it have any meaning to me." She still felt sick to her stomach. "Professor Bowman? Have you ever seen this poem before?" Bakker stared hard at him.

"No."

"That's it. Wanna go out on a limb and say if this could be by Emily Dickinson?"

"She wrote hundreds of poems and I don't know them all but the writing is similar to the way she wrote her poems." He was more concerned about Kori. She was still pale though she seemed more composed. "Detective does Kori need to stay much longer?"

Bakker considered his options and decided he could live with questioning her more tomorrow. He would've liked the chance to question Elliot for a while but figured he could wait too. As far as he knew Elliot hadn't moved all night from the bar. Besides, he could help sort out the others still upstairs with Evan.

"Okay. Miss Chandler you can go home. I'm assuming you're taking her home Professor?"

"Yes."

"I'll call you later Friday morning and we can talk more. I'm going to post a cruiser outside you're house tonight. Try and get some sleep Miss Chandler."

"Thank you Detective. I'm sorry I've been so short with you. And after all this please call me Kori. Good night."

"Good night."

Elliot stopped by his townhouse, grabbed some clothes and took Kori back to her house. He made her sit in the car while he went in and made sure nobody was in the house. Harley greeted him at the door and followed him from room to room. Elliot was sure Harley thought he was nuts. He got his bag from the car and walked in with Kori.

"Why don't you go take a nice long hot bath and I'll bring you up a glass of wine in a minute."

Kori smiled as best she could. "Thanks. That sounds like the best ending for this day." She threw her coat on the sofa and headed up the stairs. She could hear Elliot rattling around in the kitchen and talking to Harley. Kori couldn't recall ever hearing him talk to the dog like she did. Maybe this was what people meant when they referred to male bonding.

She ran the water for a bath and poured in half the bottle of bubble bath, tied her hair back and slipped into tranquility. For the moment she cleared her mind of everything and let the water and bubbles wash over her. Elliot came in with Harley in tow five minutes later.

"Are you relaxed yet?" He handed her a glass of wine and sat down on the toilet. She assumed he intended to stay and she almost laughed. All this time and all she needed was a stalker to get him in the same room with her while she was naked. And then she thought about what Paige had said and wondered if she should stand up and see what he would do. This time she did laugh. "Was that a dumb question to ask?"

"No I was just thinking about something Paige had said. I wonder if Detective Bakker let everyone go yet?"

"I can't see how he could keep them long. Don't worry about that now you're supposed to be relaxing."

"I am but I'm still concerned about my friends."

"I'm not saying you can't be concerned but you can do that later. Have some wine."

"Well maybe when I get out I'll give Paige a call."

"You might interrupt her beauty sleep."

"Huh. I'd bet she's still there, ranting and raving to one of the detectives about keeping her."

And there the two of them sat, in silence, in her bathroom, drinking wine. Kori wasn't sure what the etiquette was for bathroom conversation but this was becoming strained. If he didn't want her thinking about the one thing that seemed to occupy the better part of her week she didn't know what else there was. Maybe this was her cue to stand up. Suddenly she wished she had a phone in the bathroom. Of course that was a stupid thought because she knew exactly what Paige would tell her to do.

"What are you thinking about?" She almost didn't ask him. Sometimes there's things better left unsaid and she worried what a man sitting in the bathroom would think about.

"You. What else would I think about?"

"You actually think about me?" Kori tried to keep a straight face but a small grin grew across her lips.

"Surprisingly I think about you quite often."

"What do you think about me?"

"In general or while you're sitting naked in a bathtub?"

"You noticed the tub? I didn't think you caught on to those subtleties."

"Kori I know I'm not moving real fast but I have my reasons. And yes, I notice everything about you. Want me to wash your back?"

It was a damn good thing she was sitting down already or she would have fallen over. Before she could answer him though the doorbell rang. Someone had worse timing than she did and whoever it was they were going to get an earful from her.

"Who's ringing my door at midnight?"

"Don't move. I'll get the door."

She wasn't going to move until she realized it could be her stalker. The last thing she wanted was to be killed in a tub full of bubbles. She got up and put on her robe. That's when she heard Paige's voice and boy did she sound pissed. Of all the people to interrupt her bathroom romance it had to be Paige.

"Elliot I need to talk to her. If this weren't important I wouldn't be here."

"From what I understand, everything is important to you Paige." Elliot was as thrilled to see Paige as he would have been to see one of the detectives.

"Elliot, please, it's been a long night."

Kori found them in the kitchen. Paige was helping herself to the wine in the refrigerator. "Do you think you two could be a little louder? Maybe we could get the police officer outside to step in here for a moment."

"Kori I need to talk to you." Paige looked at Elliot, "Alone."

"I guess this can't wait till morning?"

"If it could I would have waited."

Kori knew there was no point in arguing. Paige would just fight with her and stay anyway. If she wanted to talk right now that's what they were going to do. "Elliot could you give us a few minutes?"

It was her house and her friend so he didn't bother to point out all his reasons not to leave and simply turned to go into the living room. "I'll go sit by the fire."

Kori walked over to him, squeezed his hand and kissed him on the cheek. "Thank you." After Elliot left she turned to Paige. "This had better be good."

"I threw Matt out of the house when I figured out he was having an affair and then I slept with Gabe."

Kori decided it must be a conspiracy and people were trying to shock her into falling over tonight. She felt as though she'd been hit by a brick and wasn't entirely sure her brain was comprehending this new information. It wasn't difficult to realize that she had been in the same room with a killer. It still had not sunk in completely that Elliot had been willing to wash her back. Matt having an affair was incomprehensible at the moment much less dealing with Gabe.

She knew she should close her mouth and stop gapping at Paige but that was another command that her brain couldn't understand immediately. Paige sat at the table with her head bent rolling her wine glass back and forth between her palms. Kori knew she was waiting for her to say something but Kori was speechless. It took her another good three minutes before she tried to speak.

"Paige you really need to work on your delivery of shocking news. I know you've always been direct but sometimes tactfulness and timing come into play."

"Sorry but my husband's never cheated on me before. I'm a little inexperienced how to tell people." Kori heard the sarcasm in her voice. She'd never seen Paige look so devastated in the years she'd known her. Kori on the other hand was quite aware what Paige was going through. She'd been in Paige's shoes many times while she was still married to Tyler. Her heart ached for her friend and hoped there was some way Paige was wrong.

"Are you absolutely sure Paige? I mean, there's no way you misinterpreted something?"

"I'm sure. And if there had been any doubt it was cleared up when he told me himself he was seeing some woman."

"Paige just start from the beginning. I'm still a little confused on all this so instead of playing twenty questions just tell me how you found all this out."

For the next hour and a half Kori listened as Paige described her marriage in the last few months. Paige told her that after they moved into the house Matt seemed to withdrawal from her a bit. Nothing that couldn't be explained away by Matt as just him feeling stressed at work. He'd told Paige it was a new client they were working with that had a lot of errors in their books and the IRS was going to investigate the company.

Paige confessed after getting the house she started thinking about having a baby. When she broached the subject with Matt, he showed no interest in the conversation. A few days later he started leaving the house early and coming home late. Again it was the new company he was working with.

It didn't occur to her until four weeks ago that Matt had never mentioned the name of the company. He'd always talked about what he was working on before so this seemed odd. She asked him one night when he got home but he said he went through some inventory in the company's warehouse and needed a shower. He promised they'd talk later. They never did. What little intimacy that was taking place finally ended three weeks ago. Around that time Matt claimed his mother had developed walking pneumonia. Matt began leaving even earlier and coming home later saying that he was stopping before and after work to cheek on his mother.

Paige reminded Kori that she had never gotten along with her mother-in-law but Kori already remembered that well. Matt's mother had always insisted Matt should never have married her and that the marriage wouldn't last. On Monday, Paige told Kori she really needed to talk to Matt so she called her mother-in-laws house. She hated to do it but didn't want to wait till Matt got home.

But when Paige dialed she heard a message saying the number had been disconnected. She redialed assuming she had dialed wrong but got the same thing. Paige could recall Matt 'supposedly ' calling his mother almost every day the week before at some point.

An old friend, Sarah, from their high school days, had moved to Newton Falls a few years ago and Paige knew she lived only a few blocks away. Paige called and told her friend a story about Matt being out of town and she needed to get a hold of his mother but the line wasn't working. Paige asked if she'd seen her around town lately.

At this point in the conversation Paige began to sob. Not just have tears rolling down her face or even a good cry but a complete breakdown into sobbing to where she couldn't talk anymore. Paige was bent over in her chair with her face in her hands. Kori knelt down on the floor in front of her and hugged Paige as hard as she could. They sat like that for a solid ten minutes before Paige could pull herself together enough to talk again.

"Kori it was the most humiliating experience of my entire life. I thought I was ready for anything. But what Sarah said left me mortified. At first Sarah didn't say anything and I knew by the silence that it was going to be bad. Thank God I sat down before she said a word." Paige began crying softly again. Kori waited for her patiently but she had the idea she really didn't want to hear what was coming next. Paige wasn't an overly emotional person and what Kori saw before her now scared her.

"Sarah said she wasn't sure what to say or if she should say anything. That maybe it was better if I talked to Matt. I told her to just go ahead and tell me. Sarah said she'd run into Matt weeks ago. He told her that we divorced and the woman with him was his new wife and they were looking for a place to live in Newton Falls."

"About the time Matt said his mother was sick she was. Apparently worse then I ever imagined or Matt ever said."

"What's wrong with her Paige?" Kori felt herself holding her breath.

"Nothing right now. She's dead."

"What?"

"From what I understand, when Matt first started leaving early and coming home late he was already seeing someone. He was actually going to see his mother at that time. She did have pneumonia and I guess that's what she died from or at least her heart gave out at the same time. Matt then moved his new woman into his mother's house. I guess he thought I'd never call there to find the number was disconnected before he could get around to telling me she was dead." Paige sighed heavily. "I know Susan and I didn't get along but he could have at least told me."

Kori knew her mouth was hanging open but was still to shocked to close it. She was just happy she could still speak. "What are you going to do now?"

"Beyond divorcing him? I don't know yet. But you know what? It late now and even though I'm not real fond of him we kind of forgot poor Elliot is in the living room. So I think I'm going to take my leave and go home."

Paige stood and grabbed her coat. Kori did feel a little bad because truth be told, she had forgotten Elliot was still here. She walked Paige to the door and as they passed the living room, they saw Harley curled up by the now dwindling fire and Elliot asleep on the sofa.

"You know Kori; he's sort of cute when he's sleeping."

"He's cute all the time."

"Maybe. I guess I'm not a very good judge of character."

"You chose me as a friend so you can't be all that bad." Kori smiled and opened the door for Paige. "And I hope you know, I'd forget Elliot anytime you need to talk."

They both laughed and Paige headed toward the drive. "Thanks for tonight Kori. I'm sorry I've been such a bitch lately."

"I doubt you're extremely sorry but you're entitled. Try and get some sleep. And call me later."

"Are you going into work today?"

"I don't know. I have a feeling I'd have to fight Elliot to let me out of the house."

"Well, maybe he's right just this once. Maybe a day off is what you need. Janine can handle it. I'll talk to you later."

She got into her car and left and Kori stood in the doorway until she couldn't see her taillights any more. She called Harley and let him out then closed the door softly and locked it. She walked into the living room and looked at Elliot. He was sleeping in a sitting position and she decided she'd just let him sleep. He'd probably pay for it in the morning with a stiff neck but he looked so peaceful.

Kori ran upstairs and got a blanket and returned to the living room. She'd had every intention of covering Elliot up and going to bed. But the idea of cuddling up with him on the sofa was too much too resist. She threw an afghan over him, put a pillow on his lap and laid her head on the pillow. Harley came and slept next to the sofa and it didn't take Kori long to fall asleep. After all this evening had brought she was still spending her first night in Elliot's arms.

He wondered if the police knew the note in the cafe was as much for their benefit as it was for Kori. He thought she was stronger and was quite surprised by her reaction. Well, things would be changing now. He wanted to get a little more personal so he wrote the note on a napkin from the cafe. Personally, he thought it was brilliant.

He would bet his life the police would sit around scratching their heads over that one. He could just see them, going over that night in the cafe, trying to remember if someone had been sitting at a table writing on anything. They thought he was that stupid.

He'd gotten the napkin from another trip when he'd stopped in the cafe. But the two purposes the note had were effective. First, he wanted the police and Kori to know he wouldn't be caught if he didn't want too. And he definitely didn't want that. This game was just getting fun and the prize for winning was too great to quit.

Second, and most important, he wanted Kori to realize they'd been in the same room together and she was fine. Not that they'd never been together before but she hadn't seen him for who he is. She would soon too. He had to clean up a few problems he hadn't anticipated on first before his greatness was revealed.

Kori still didn't seem to understand. She continued to surround herself with those beneath her, she needed more proof of his greatness and her uniqueness.

Yes, they would be together but first he had to show Kori how wrong some people were for her. The sight of Kori together with someone so unworthy was almost unbearable. He had wanted to scream as he watched them together. He needed to rid her life of those unworthy of her. And he would begin now.

But before his game continued in that direction he needed to make a phone call.

CHAPTER 6

Kori awoke Friday morning at eight o'clock to an empty house. She found a note from Elliot saying he had classes that morning and that he would call her around noon. He was obviously assuming she wasn't going into work. Kori started a pot of coffee and went to the bathroom. The phone rang and she guessed Elliot was calling earlier than planned or Janine was wondering if she was coming in today.

She answered on the third ring. "Hello?" There was no reply. The Caller ID was no help either. The number came up "unknown". "Hello?" She was about to hang up when she heard her name whispered very softly. Her heart was beating a little faster and she was taking shorter breaths.

"Hello? Is someone there?" She held her breath.

"Yes." The voice was almost lost to her. Kori wasn't sure if she'd heard it or not.

"Listen, I think this is a bad connection. I can't hear you well. I'm going to hang up so if you're not a salesman call back."

"Two down."

Again the voice was little more than a whisper in the wind. Kori knew it was him. She wanted to hang up but she was also afraid to end the call too. "What do you want?" Her heart was beating so fast now it sounded like she had a freight train running through her. She felt herself holding her breath again and exhaled before she passed out.

"Two to go."

She was about to ask what he meant but then she heard a click and then the dial tone. It was his game and he had decided to end it. Kori stood looking at the phone wondering what she was supposed to do now. Detective Bakker was the first logical thought that caught her attention. She replaced the phone and scrambled through her purse to find his card. Kori figured if ever there was a time to use his cell phone number now would be good. She dialed and waited for him to answer.

Jonah and Evan had met at the police station at seven in the morning. For the past hour they sat going over the interviews from the following night. Jonah had the feeling they had both missed something that night but couldn't put his finger on it. Evan wasn't entirely sure Jonah was right.

"Okay, so this note shows up and you're telling me you don't think we missed something?"

"No, not necessarily." Evan knew he was getting to Jonah and Evan was enjoying himself to no end. The crease between Jonah's eyes was deeper than Evan had ever seen and his jaw was set.

"Could you expand on that idea of yours?"

"Jonah that note could have been written at any time."

"And put in the envelope and left that night." Jonah could see where he was going.

"That way, he wasn't sitting at the cafe writing and looking obvious."

"Then obviously he's been to the cafe before Thursday night to get a napkin."

"We're already assuming Kori knows this guy. It wouldn't be a huge leap."

"Only one problem Evan. How'd the note end up on the floor without being seen till closing time?"

Evan had thought of the same thing. He would have liked to think he or Jonah would have seen someone drop the envelope on the floor but he wasn't so sure. He and Jonah had each made separate trips to the bar. Someone could have dropped that envelope at any time when only one of them was watching the entire place. It could have slipped from a pocket very easily and he said as much to Jonah.

Jonah considered this for a moment. "So what's to say he wasn't sitting at a table?"

"Nothing really. But I don't think so."

"So let's assume it's Elliot Bowman. Then what? He never moved from the bar last night."

"His student's look up to him. He could have asked one for a favor or even paid one of them to drop an envelope. A kid wouldn't think twice about it."

"And Gabe Hathaway? He didn't move either." Jonah could feel them slipping into good cop, bad cop rolls. Or maybe this was Devil's Advocate he was playing.

"He went to the bathroom once. Could have dropped it then."

"And Boyd Thomas just happened to be sitting at one of the tables." Jonah said.

"Yep. How easy would that have been? So all three are still plausible."

"I don't know. Seems that way. Hold that thought. I'll be right back." Jonah got up and walked to the bathroom. He liked the scenario of Boyd Thomas but it seemed almost too easy. Nearly a week had gone by since they found the body of Shelly Roberts and they still didn't have a decent clue. A strong motive was also lacking which was driving him crazy. What was it about Kori Chandler that got this guys attention?

Jonah's cell phone rang as he stepped out the door. "Bakker."

"Detective, this is Kori Chandler. I think I just had a conversation with our poet."

"Give me ten minutes." Jonah hung up as he reached his desk and looked at Evan. "Let's take a ride over Kori's."

"Why? What's up?"

"That was her on the phone. Says she just got a call from the killer."

"No shit. That's a new twist."

The patrol car Jonah had sitting in front of Kori's house was still parked there when he and Evan arrived. Kori opened the door when she saw them get out of the car. The first thing he noticed was that she was one of those people that still managed to look attractive even in the worst circumstances. The second thing he noticed was she was holding a lit cigarette, which he'd never seen her with before.

"Morning Kori. Didn't know you smoked? New habit?"

"Old one. My stress relief for the morning."

They walked inside and went to sit at her kitchen table. They accepted her offer for coffee and after she sat down Jonah asked her about the call. Kori told them about the short conversation and she thought Detective Harding looked more irritated than usual.

Harding was staring at her intently. "But you can't identify the voice?"

"No. I told you it was brief and he talked just above a whisper. It was difficult to hear him much less determine if he sounded familiar."

"Do you know where Professor Bowman is?"

"Teaching a class I believe."

Evan got up from his seat, took out his cell phone and went outside. Jonah and Kori both knew he was calling Elliot and Jonah assumed he'd make the same phone call to a few other people. The kitchen was filled with quiet tension until Kori broke the silence. "Detective Bakker? Do you think he killed someone else?"

Jonah thought about what Kori had told them from the phone conversation. Two down, two to go. If that did mean he killed somebody he's planning on more. "I don't know but it's possible." Jonah watched the look of horror pass across her face. As Evan came back in he glanced at Jonah and then turned to Kori. In his most fatherly tone of voice he said; "Miss Chandler I don't want you to leave this house until we get back. The patrol car is still outside and will remain there. If the phone rings and the number isn't known don't answer it. Is there someone who could come and sit with you?"

"Paige McCleary might."

"Fine. Call her to come over and don't answer the door for anyone but her or one of us. Do you understand that?"

"Yes."

"I'm not sure yet but I don't want to take any chances. Just sit tight until we get back."

And they were gone. Kori didn't know if the phone call was more frightening or the way Detective Harding was acting and talking. She called Paige's house and prayed she'd be up and could come over. Kori didn't want to think what Harding would do if he came back and she was alone.

Paige's sleepy voice answered on the sixth ring. "This had better be good."

"Paige I need a favor."

"What?"

She was definitely not a morning person either. "I need you to come over."

"When?"

"Now."

"Now? Kori do you have any idea what time it is? I thought only wildlife were awake at this hour?"

"Paige I got a phone call this morning. I think it was the killer."

"Did you call those detectives?" If she had any thought of rolling over and going back to sleep the idea was gone now.

"Yeah. They were here and left. Detective Harding wants someone to come sit with me. Why I don't know but I'm not going to argue with him either."

"Okay just give me twenty minutes."

Jonah knew by the way Evan was talking to Kori he was on to something good. "So what'd you find out?"

Evan went to the driver's side of the car and got in. "Well, first I called Bowman but he wasn't in his office. I'm leaving that alone for the time being. We can always check if he was in class or not. Then I called Boyd Thomas at the car lot only to find he hasn't arrived in this morning yet but supposedly that's not all that unusual. Then I tried the number Hathaway gave you and got his voice mail."

"So where are we going?"

"I thought we'd cruise by Hathaway's and see if he's home. If the trucks gone he could be anywhere. Then I thought we'd see why Mr. Thomas has decided to sleep in today."

"Evan? Have you given anymore thought to what Kori said the killer told her?"

"About two down?"

"Yeah. It's registered in the brain but I don't want to start making assumptions. Maybe he's referring to Shelly Roberts."

"Evan we need to think about it now. If someone other than Roberts is dead then he's planning two more. We're not going to have much time to narrow down three suspects."

"I know but this could be a bluff. This guy has so far gone to great lengths for Kori not to discover his identity. Don't you think this call was kind of risky?"

"Maybe."

Evan knew there was more to it than that. "What the hell kind of answer is that? Maybe? How about expanding your thoughts on that."

"Technically, we need three murders to classify him as a 'serial killer'. But that just doesn't fit this guy. Michelle Roberts was tied to that tree like an offering. And with the notes, I'd say his offering was to Kori Chandler. This guy is probably obsessed with Kori. If he is, the Roberts girl and the first two notes are meant for her. Like he's showing off his skills and talents. The third note seems to address us more than Kori. So if he's killed again what in hell is his motive? Are we getting closer to him than we know or is he pissed off about something? Again, if he's pissed off, the phone call makes sense. He's angry and he wants Kori to know it."

Jonah thought about it for the rest of the ride. If they had a pissed off killer on their hands, that may just be worse than if he were a serial killer. At least they could profile a serial killer. And what if they were getting closer to him and he was getting nervous. That could be just as bad for them and Kori than anything else.

Evan tried not to think about it as they reached Boyd Thomas' drive. He wanted a clear head when they interviewed this asshole. Besides, all the 'what ifs' were starting to give him a headache. They both got out of the car and walked to the front entrance of the townhouse Boyd owned.

Jonah tried to see in the garage. "Frosted windows. I can't be sure but it looks like there's the outline of a car in there." He knocked on the door and waited. When no answer came he tried the doorbell. After a minute he rang the bell again and pounded on the door. "Mr. Thomas. Detective Bakker from Tabor Police. I'd like to speak to you."

Evan went around to the side of the house and peered into the window. No lights were on inside and it was difficult for Harding's eyes to adjust. He could see some light filtering in from a back window but could only see shadows. "Jonah I'm going to see if I can get a look in a back window." He headed toward the back and was surprised to see a backdoor with a small deck off it. Evan could still hear Jonah pounding away on the front door.

There was a mini blind covering the window on the door but the blind was slightly askew at the top. Standing on the tip of his toes he could just see into the kitchen. What he saw told him someone in that house either had one hell of a party or one nasty fight. "Jonah. Have a look in the window."

Jonah glanced around the kitchen and then turned to Evan. "I think we need to open that door."

"No argument from me." With that, they tried the door and found it locked. Evan took out his gun and with the butt of it knocked out a single pane. He reached in and unlocked the door. They stepped into a kitchen that was trashed. A small table was pushed against the wall. If two chairs belonged there than one was missing. They're feet crunched broken glass that hadn't come from the pane Evan broke. The mini blind above the kitchen window was pulled up on one end and then they both noticed the large stain on the floor.

"Are you thinking what I am?" Evan had seen enough blood in his time to know that looked like a large amount on the kitchen floor.

"Looks like blood. Also looks like drag marks leading into the other room. And do you smell something?"

"Besides the metallic sent of blood?" They stared toward the doorway leading out of the kitchen. It led to a dining room/ living room combination. Stairs that would take you to the second floor could be seen. And there was an obvious dragline of blood right up to the stairs. "To much blood for whoever was bleeding to live." Jonah knew it before Evan said a word. If that blood came from Boyd Thomas, Jonah was certain he was dead.

As they carefully approached the steps going up, the line continued. Though it was much less a line now but more like a splatter of blood on each step. "Smells getting worse." Evan heartedly agreed with Jonah's statement. "Looks like someone was dragged feet first up the stairs." They made their way up trying not to step where the killer would have had to. The bloodline was less visible now but still evident. It ended at the second door on the right.

Bakker and Harding had kept their guns drawn as they followed the path upstairs but as they looked behind door number two they knew it was unnecessary. They lowered their weapons and looked at what used to be Boyd Thomas. Evan made the call to report it as Jonah walked into the room. He heard Evan saying paramedics would not be needed. Jonah stood staring at the body knowing nothing would ever help Boyd.

Boyd Thomas was propped up in the king-size bed. Each hand had been tied to knobs on the headboard along with each foot tied to separate ends of the footboard. A small hole in his throat could be seen and Jonah guessed the deathblow was to the back of the throat. Possibly a knife that went from the back and punctured the front of the throat.

Masking tape was covering Boyd's mouth and a piece was placed over each eye. His fingers had also been taped. Then he noticed the edge of what looked like paper sticking out from under Boyd's shirt. "Evan. Come here a sec." As Evan walked over to Jonah's side he pointed to the bottom of Boyd's t-shirt. "Does that look like paper sticking out to you?"

Evan held his breath and bent forward to get a better look. "If it's not, Boyd had some strange practices." Jonah slipped on a pair of latex gloves and slowly lifted the shirt. The small, block letters were clearly visible. "Son of bitch." Evan couldn't have said it better. They knew they were in trouble now. This guy was definitely pissed about something.

"Can you read it?" Evan didn't want to get any closer than he had too and since Jonah was already there he'd let Jonah do the hard work.

"Some. Blood's got on some of it. I think I'd rather wait. I don't think there's any evidence I'd destroy but you never know, we may get lucky some day." Jonah was still standing over Boyd when the odd smell hit him again. Looking at Evan he said, "And what in hell is that odor?"

They had been concentrating on Boyd and Evan almost forgot the smell. It was obnoxious. And then he noticed the door off the bedroom. "I'd say the source is behind that door." Jonah turned to see where Evan was pointing. They looked at each other for a moment and decided they would both go and look.

As they pushed the door open slowly, the stench assaulted them. Jonah registered gasoline first and then the distinct odor of flesh. They saw the body in the tub simultaneously but only an autopsy would be able to determine if it was male or female. Jonah swore under his breath.

They made a quick guess that the body was doused with gasoline while in the tub. Evan pointed to the wall opposite the tub and the fire extinguisher. "Looks like our killer waited for the body to burn and then put the fire out."

An hour later, Bakker and Harding stood outside Boyd's townhouse knowing their luck hadn't changed. Kori had to be called but neither one were looking forward to telling her. After the note was removed from the body and bagged as evidence they got to read it. And they could tell right away this one was different. This one had a force about it that made it more personal than ever. Evan and Jonah knew their time was short on solving this case. And they both understood Kori's life would depend on it.

"Are you just going to stare at the phone all day or are you going to call her?"

"Yeah I'll call but I'd like to drive over there too. I want her to hear this poem."

When the phone rang, Paige and Kori froze for an instant. They waited to see if a number appeared on the Caller ID. Kori remembered she could breath when she saw Bakker's name and number. "Hello?" At first, there was no response and she felt a coldchill cover her body. "Kori? It's Bakker. You okay over there?"

"I'm fine. Paige came to sit with me. Did you find anything?"

"I'll talk to you when we get there. We should be there in about fifteen minutes."

Paige watched her hang up the phone and sit back down. "I take it that was Detective Bakker?"

"Yep. He said they should be here in a few minutes."

"Whose 'they'? Is Detective Harding with him?"

"He was earlier so I guess he's still with Bakker."

Paige waited but when Kori didn't say any more she couldn't help but ask, "So? Did they find any body?"

"He wouldn't say. Said he'd talk to me when he got here."

Kori could see the disappointment on Paige's face. Patience was not one of her best qualities. But she had done her job well today. She'd managed to occupy Kori's time and kept the conversation light. They hadn't speculated on who the supposed killer might be and Paige never brought up Matt. Kori was surprised the conversation never included Elliot or Tyler either.

They had talked mostly about childhood and their early days in school together. Thinking about it now, Kori realized they never talked about high school but had they Tyler and Matt would have to be dragged into the conversation. Kori knew Paige wouldn't allow that this morning.

Bakker and Harding arrived within his estimated time and neither looked happy. Kori wanted to believe Bakker could have a bad day that had nothing to do with her. But good news just didn't look like it was on the itinerary for the day. She led the detectives to the kitchen and poured them each a cup of coffee.

Once they were all seated, Bakker looked at her intently. "Kori are you absolutely sure you didn't know Michelle Roberts?" There was the slightest hint of desperation in his voice that unnerved her. She was beginning to think about going to her bed and staying there until this was all over but that wouldn't help either.

"I'm positive I didn't know her. I'm not saying she never came into the cafe and I didn't run into her but if I did I don't remember her. And I never knew her personally."

"Well, I hate to tell you this Kori but your admirer just made this very personal. Boyd Thomas and, we think his girlfriend, were murdered last night in his home."

Though she would never have married him, Kori knew in that one instant his words registered that she loved Boyd more than she would ever have admitted to herself under normal circumstances. At times he could be a jerk but he had treated her well and had loved her. She understood he was gone but she was having a hard time grasping the idea she would never see him again.

Kori could see Bakker watching her. She'd heard Paige mumble something but now Paige was sitting with her head bowed, starring at the floor. Harding was holding a piece of paper in one hand and rolling a pen between the fingers of his other hand. She tried to think of something, anything to say just so the kitchen wasn't so quiet. "Did he leave a note?"

Evan took the paper he was holding and slid it over to Kori. "This is a copy of the note left. The original was bagged and left as evidence." That wasn't entirely the truth but he and Jonah decided showing Kori a bloodstained note was unnecessary.

Kori took the paper and read the poem four times trying to digest the words. Even though it was written in a different handwriting, she could still see it as it had been. Printed in small block letters.

> Ambition cannot find him.
> Affection doesn't know
> How many leagues of nowhere
> Lies between them now.

All three of them were now watching her. Finally, she gave the paper to Paige. She should have known how bad the news was going to be just by the presence of Paige. Neither detective even hinted for Paige to leave. Then she remembered something Bakker had said that was still bothering her. "What did you mean when you referred to this animal as 'my admirer'?"

Jonah glanced at Evan, gave a little shrug and figured he might as well tell her his theory. "I think this is a case of stalking that's beginning to escalate. I think this guy has been watching you for a while now. The picture of Shelly Roberts was taken in the summer and her parents told us she decided to stay in town over the summer and work a retail job. If this guy were taking her picture in the summer he had to have known what he would eventually do to her."

Paige finally decided to join in on the conversation. "What's to say he wasn't dating her and just took her picture for the hell of it. Maybe they got into a fight, broke it off and he became fixed on Kori?"

Evan answered her. "Her parents said she wasn't dating anyone. And I know kids don't tell their parents every thing but her roommate and other friend's support that she wasn't dating. I can see the parents not knowing but I would find it very odd that a twenty-year-old girl wouldn't say a word to friends."

"What else makes you think this is a stalking?" Kori could see Bakker had given some thought to this and she needed to hear it all.

"The way the body was tied up was almost like a 'offering' for lack of a better term. Sort of like he wanted to give you something. Show you how devoted he is. And then he kills you're ex-boyfriend. So far all the notes seem to be talking about him or have a reference to him. This one is different. It's personal. And this note is the first to directly talk about emotion. I think something with Boyd really pissed him off." They opted not to discuse the body in the tub. She was upset enough and they weren't even positive who was in the tub.

"I kissed him." Kori said it so slowly and quietly, Bakker wasn't sure he heard her right.

"I'm sorry. What did you say?"

"When he was leaving the cafe last night. We were saying goodbye and I leaned over and we kissed each other on the cheek. This monster must have been watching the whole time. I might as well have killed him myself."

"Kori you can't think that way. You can't be sure he was watching last night. He's probably been obsessed with you for a while. If it is someone you already know, he may be getting ticked off you can't see how much he loves you. Taking out you're ex-boyfriend doesn't sound far-fetched if he started watching you while you were still dating him."

Panic swarmed over her. "Well if he's pissed about an old flame what's he going to think about a new one? Does that mean Elliot could be next? Is that what you mean? Is that what he meant about two more to go?" Before she could block the question, it rolled though her mind. If Boyd got killed just because they once dated and she kissed him the other night what would he do to Elliot?

She had to calm down but still, fear griped her. Taking slow, deep breaths, she lowered her head and tried to get control of her feelings. That was the first time she noticed Harley was gone. When Paige arrived, Harley had taken his spot on the rug in front of the kitchen sink. He'd walked with her to let the detectives in but she couldn't recall when he disappeared. She hadn't thought much about him until this moment and then caught sight of him in the dining room.

He must have sensed she was upset because now he whined once and she could see one eye peering at her from around the corner. They watched each other for what seemed an eternity. Finally, he let out one 'woof' and headed to the back door. Normally, Kori opened the door and he would fly down the steps as though he knew a rabbit was waiting for a chase.

But just like hers, his routines had also changed. Since Sunday morning, Harley would watch her open the door and then just sit and stare at her. She'd finally tell him it was okay and he'd poke his head out the door and gingerly walk down the stairs. Kori wondered if Harley knew who the killer was and their staring match a few minutes ago was his way of trying to connect with her on some level. Or maybe he just wanted to see how long it took her to figure out he had to pee.

When Kori turned back to the table, Bakker was still watching her. Harding and Paige seemed to be lost in their own thoughts but Bakkers thoughts were directly on her. Kori sat down and sighed.

Looking at Bakker, she said, "So what do I do now? Sit in my house till you two catch his guy? Should I tell all my friends to stay in also?"

Jonah set his jaw and thought carefully about what he was about to say. He didn't want to scare her anymore than she already was but he wanted to drive home his point. "Kori you don't have to give up your life just be more aware of what's around you. I'm going to post a patrol car with you around the clock. And I would prefer if you not close up or leave the cafe alone anymore."

He could see she didn't like to be told what to do, especially when it came to work, but this had to be done. "Kori whoever this guy is, he's smart. So far, we've got nothing for evidence. Do you understand what I'm saying? This guy is cleaning up before he leaves. We have no hair, fiber or fingerprints. The rope and knife used on Shelly Roberts could have been picked up at any hardware store and we have three of them right here in Tabor. The paper the notes are written on is generic."

"So what you're saying is he's like a phantom. He can do whatever he pleases, for no apparent reason, and he has nothing to fear from the police? You're not making me feel very safe Detective."

"Kori, I am trying to keep you safe. I think Shelly Roberts was killed to get your attention. The notes, I believe are the killers' ways of letting you and us know he hasn't gone away. And to some extent he wants you to feel as though he has twenty-four hour access to you. Boyd's murder feels more personal. He was pissed about something with you and Boyd. I want to make him believe he still has access to you while in reality, we slowly stop him."

"Why slowly?"

Paige had been so quiet until she asked the question, Bakker and Kori had almost forgot about her. Evan decided to take his place in the conversation now too. He said, "Because of Boyd. If this guy has been watching Kori since summer like we suspect, he may be getting tired of playing games. Kori still doesn't know who he is and that might frustrate him."

"You think he wants Kori to know him?" Paige was amazed. "Why would anyone go through this much to conceal an identity he really wants known?"

Evan continued to answer Paige. "That would be the final piece of the puzzle. Why else go to these lengths and never have your identity known? He wants Kori for himself and he'll probably do anything to get her."

Kori was starting to have that odd sensation that she wasn't in the room at all. Evan and Paige were talking about someone she was related to but not her. How could she possibly miss a guy that's been watching her for months? "Bakker, I don't get it."

"Get what?" He felt as confused as she looked.

"You guys keep referring to him as a stalker but he sounds more like a psychopath. I thought most people who were stalked could tell you who it was that was stalking them? And I thought stalkers killed the person they were stalking not everyone around them?"

Jonah sighed heavily. "Look Kori, I'm not sure what a stalker is supposed to do but I know what this one is doing. All I know is the best way to keep you safe right now is to have you stay in one place. There's a cop out front and I'd like someone in here with you at all times. As soon as I have more information I'll let you know."

The phone rang and Kori jumped. She thought she had a grip on herself but one jingle from the phone and she was a basket case. Her nerves were fried and now they all knew it. She saw Elliot's number on the display window and answered.

"Hi. Thought I'd check in with you real quick. I have a meeting in ten minutes. So how are you?"

"Well, since you asked, let me tell you about my morning."

Kori went on autopilot and filled Elliot in on the morning news in five minutes. He waited till she finished and then told her he'd be over as soon as his meeting was done to relieve Paige. She didn't bother to argue with him or tell him she was 'fine' but chose to accept his company. Bakker and the others were still sitting at her table when she hung up the phone.

Jonah spoke first. "Was that Professor Bowman?"

"Yes." Kori knew where this was going before Bakker said another word.

"Do you happen to know where he was last night or this morning?"

"Actually, Elliot fell asleep on my couch last night and left this morning."

"What time did he leave?"

"I got up at eight and he was gone." As she said it even Kori didn't like the way it sounded.

"And is he still at the college now?"

"Yes. He has a meeting and then he'll be over."

As Jonah and Evan stood to leave, Kori heard Harley at the back door. "Kori, you let Harley in and I'll walk them out." Paige was on her feet and seemed eager to get them out.

"Kori we'll let you know if anything develops."

"Thanks. To both of you."

Paige led the way to the door and as Jonah walked out she stopped Evan at the doorway. "Could I ask you a favor Detective?"

"Sure. What can I do for you?"

"The next time you have a few free moments, could you stop by my house?"

"Well, I have a few right now."

Paige looked back at the kitchen and then back at Evan. "No. I'd rather talk to you alone."

"Okay. I'll try later tonight if that's all right with you? Do you want me to call first?"

"It doesn't matter."

Harding simply nodded and left. Paige went back to the kitchen to find Kori sitting on the floor rubbing Simon's belly. Kori looked up at her and said, "So what was that all about?"

Paige put on her most innocent face and asked, "What do you mean?"

"Oh come on Paige. You damn near broke your neck getting them to the door."

"Kori I just wanted them out of here. You need some time to think about everything that's happened and you know as well as I do that Bakker would have continued to question you until he left."

"Hey, if you don't want to tell me that's fine. But I guess the line of bull you just gave me could be true too." Kori was in no mood to get into an argument with Paige.

"So Elliot's coming over later?"

"Yeah. Soon as he finishes up at school he'll come to relieve you."

"Granted this isn't the most pleasant reason to be together but I don't think you have to say it like he's doing me some kind of favor by coming here so I can leave."

Kori could tell Paige was going to develop an attitude now. Usually when she did this it was to cover up her true feelings. Kori wanted to know what Paige had said to the detectives but had learned long ago if Paige wanted her to know Paige would tell her. Obviously that wasn't going to happen. They sat quietly in the kitchen drinking coffee for the next half-hour.

Kori had thought about asking Paige about Matt or more importantly, about Paige sleeping with Gabe but neither subject seemed appropriate to Paige's mood. She decided to lie down on the couch till Elliot arrived. Paige was not a good companion now so sleep seemed the likely choice. Her sleep was restless at best and her dreams were that of monsters and phone calls, dead bodies and the men she'd loved. She dreamed of Elliot and Boyd and oddly, of Tyler.

When Bakker and Harding left Kori's house, Bakker started the car and began to drive as though he had a destination in mind. Evan stared for a minute but when he realized Jonah had no intention of telling him were they were heading he asked.

"So do you mind telling me who we're going to see or should I guess?"

"Amuse me. Guess."

"Ummm, Professor Bowman?"

"Not very amusing Evan but good guess."

"Do you really think he had the time to kill Boyd and get to school to have an alibi?"

"Evan we have no idea what time he left Kori's this morning. If he left at four or five in the morning then he'd have had plenty of time."

"And the motive?"

"I've thought for a while now that we're dealing with a stalking case. I did some research on stalkers. Most stalkers are men and have a higher intelligence then other criminals. They're likely to have psychiatric problems and may have a past history of it. Or a past history of other criminal behavior or substance abuse. And most have a personality disorder like paranoid, dependent, borderline or narcissistic."

"And what do you think our stalker suffers from?"

"Narcissism."

"And why is that?"

"Basic signs of stalking is persistent phone calls, threats, sending gifts and sending written notes along with many other behaviors. There are basically three types of stalkers. Love obsessional, Erotomania, and Simple Obsessional with the last being the most popular. With the Simple Obsessional, some type of relationship exists between the victim and the stalker. But the connection can range from lover to acquaintance and even a customer."

"So the killer could be Bowman or a customer at the cafe that Kori never even met? But, if it's not Bowman, why's a stranger killing? I can understand Boyd, an ex-boyfriend, but still can't figure Shelly."

"I think they're his gifts to Kori."

"And he's sending written notes with the gifts."

"Exactly. But I think Boyd is presenting us with another problem. Eventually, some stalkers begin objectification, which would be this stalkers way of seeing Kori as an object."

"And seeing her as an object he feels no empathy for her."

"You got it."

"And let me guess again. Being narcissistic will only exaggerate the stalking behavior."

"You're on a role Evan. Narcissists feel superior to others, entitled, uses others to meet their own needs and show no empathy."

They were sitting outside the building that housed Elliot Bowman's office. "So what's our next move?"

"Well, he won't feel that privileged because there are two other people on my list but I think it's time to inform Professor Bowman that he is now officially a suspect in two murders and a stalking case."

"This is not going to go over well."

"Evan, I hope you're right. I'd like to see Elliot Bowman lose control for just a second."

CHAPTER 7

Paige arrived home around two o'clock. She walked into the yellow kitchen and decided right then and there that the kitchen would be next on the remodeling list. It crossed her mind that it might be best to wait and see what happened with Matt but then again he surely hadn't put his life on hold for anything. She would call Gabe in the morning and see about scheduling the kitchen for renovation.

Knowing Elliot was with Kori now; Paige felt she could relax on that stress front for the night. She walked over to the refrigerator and was immediately reminded that she hadn't shopped for food in some time. Splurging for the evening, she grabbed a bottle of beer and plopped down on a kitchen chair. Between Kori being stalked, Matt having an affair, her having a fling with Gabe, and the awful color of the room, she wanted to scream.

Paige thought seriously for a moment on that idea. She didn't know anybody who ever said they wanted to scream and were stupid enough to do it. The act of screaming could potentially release the pent up feeling of stress she was experiencing and thought she might give it a try. Who would ever know? A knock on the front door stopped her and her thoughts jumped to Matt. He couldn't possibly still see this as his home so why wouldn't he knock?

As she walked to the door, every nerve in her body seemed to stand on end. She tensed for what she assumed would be a yelling match and she was definitely in the mood for it. Maybe yelling would be as therapeutic as screaming at the top of her lungs. But when she flung the door open it wasn't Matt standing before her.

Paige was shocked to find a smiling Detective Harding standing in front of her. Her mouth slightly a gap, it took a moment before she stammered out a greeting. "Hi." was about all she could manage and that seemed to make the detective smile even larger.

Evan guessed from her expression that she was expecting someone else and he had caught her by surprise. The thought of surprising her made him grin wider. "Hi. You asked me to stop when I had a free moment. I know I said evening so if this is a bad time I could come back?"

"No, now is fine. I'm sorry. Come in." She felt like an ass and probably looked the part too.

"I got the impression that whatever you wanted to talk about was important. Who's staying with Kori now?"

"Elliot came over as soon as he could." She was going to take him to the kitchen and then remembered the state of it and headed into the living room. "Can I get you anything to drink? I could make some coffee if you'd like?"

"No I'm fine, thanks."

"So I guess you want to get right down to business and know why I asked you here?"

"Well, you've definitely got my curiosity peeked. But you can take your time. I've nowhere to be right now." Evan had the distinct feeling this was going to be difficult for her. Her hair was still braided and she continued to stand after he had taken a seat. She was rubbing her hands together so hard he was waiting to see if a spark would come from them. It didn't take long before the pacing began.

"You see a lot of things have been happening in my life and I've been doing a lot of thinking lately. I think some things that have happened to me may tie into what Kori is going through."

Evan furrowed his brow and stared intently at Paige. "How so?"

"Recently I found out that my husband, Matt, has been having an affair. That in itself wouldn't make me want to question his motives since his motives seem pretty obvious. What bother's me is the ease with which he did it. It's not that he's just sleeping with someone else. He's built a whole other life."

"Exactly what kind of other life?"

"Well, his mother died and he never told me. He simply moved his new love into his mother's house and told people we were already divorced."

"And how does this tie into Kori?"

She took a deep breath. "You would have to talk with whoever this other woman is but as far as I know, I can't account for many nights Matt was gone. What he's done is not the man that I've known and loved for years. If he's capable of lying to such an extent to me what else is he capable of? And no, I'm not being vindictive or anything like that. You and Detective Bakker keep suggesting that the man who's after Kori is someone close to her. Someone that could watch her and not be suspicious at the same time. Matt has known Kori since high school. He knows her house, her work, her schedule, and how she reacts to stress. And Matt's normal habits started to change around April."

Evan sat quietly listening to her. What she was describing was the exact picture of what they were looking for but he could also hear the pain in her voice. He didn't believe she was doing this out of spite for her husband's indiscretions but, again, it almost seemed too easy.

He cleared his throat before speaking and when he did speak he used the softest tone he could. "I know this must have been difficult for you to tell me. I will look into this. Thank you. And please don't worry about it. I'll let you know if anything comes of this."

"Thanks for listening. And please know I'm not doing this to get even with him or anything. My marriage is obviously over, but Kori's life isn't, and I'll help her any way I can."

Evan nodded his head, smiled and said, "I'll call you in a couple of days."

Paige watched him go and couldn't decide whether or not she played the part of an ass completely or only half way. She went through the conversation in her mind and it all seemed so surreal. Did she really just turn in her husband's name as the possible stalker? And he told her not to worry. Yeah, right. God only knew what Matt was going to do if the police approached him but she would deal with that later. She just needed to occupy her time right now. Maybe she'd call Gabe now instead of in the morning. Paige went in search of the phone.

Evan left Paige's house with the intention of heading straight to the police station where Jonah was waiting for him. They'd decided to question Gabe Hathaway again in light of Boyd's death along with Elliot, which they'd done earlier. But Evan found himself driving around town trying to sort out what Paige had told him. He wasn't sure whether it was exactly what she'd said or something in his subconscious that was sparked by the conversation but he had an uneasy feeling. 'Uneasy' was as close as he could come to putting a name to it and when he felt this way he knew from experience he was missing something.

Evan knew Matt McCleary as an acquaintance, which didn't mean much, but he never struck Evan as the kind of guy to terrorize a woman. Of course, Paige probably never expected him to be the kind to cheat on her either but cheating and killing were two different worlds. Maybe that was what was irritating him. How does a wife go from having a cheating husband to accusing him or even suggesting, that he was the monster in her best friends' nightmares?

Harding arrived at the station twenty minutes later and headed to his desk on the second floor. Jonah was hunched over the computer at his desk and it took him a minute to notice Evan had sat down. Evan sat quietly staring out the windows opposite his desk. He knew Jonah had stopped whatever he was doing and was now looking at him and waiting for him to tell him what happened but he still wasn't sure what occurred at Paige's.

"Well?" Jonah leaned back in his chair and waited some more.

"What?"

"Don't be coy Evan it doesn't suit you at all. What happened with Paige?"

"She offered her estranged husband up for inspection in the Chandler case."

Jonah raised his eyebrows. "No shit. Now that's interesting. Didn't know they were estranged. Sounds like she's trying to get back at him or did he have a thing for Kori we don't know about?"

Evan told him about Matt McCleary's 'other' life and that Paige couldn't account for his whereabouts. Jonah listened but still wasn't making the connection. "So she's married to a cheating secret agent.

How does that make him a killer or a stalker? Did he ever show any interest in Kori?

"I'm guessing that in her mind, if he can lie about another woman he's capable of anything. As far as I know any interest in Kori is general."

"General because Paige and Kori are friends. Well, couldn't hurt to talk to him. The other woman should be able to verify if he was with her or not"

Evan had such a distant look in his eye Jonah wondered if Evan had even heard what he just said. "What do you think?" Again there was no response from him. "Evan? You still with me?"

Evan jumped a little and sat a little straighter in his chair. "Sorry. Got lost in my thoughts."

"Well, you wanna share those thoughts?"

"Not really but I will. Bear with me and try and follow. As far as suspects go we've been looking at Boyd Thomas, Bowman, Hathaway and to some extent Tyler Adams. Except for Hathaway all the others have lived here for some time or for their entire lives. Even Matt McCleary fits into that statement." Evan paused for a moment trying to get his thoughts into a clear picture. "Since I've talked to Paige something about all this has been bothering me. I think it's the idea that one of them is stalking Kori. I think stalking is the wrong word. Killer is accurate but I don't think this guy is stalking."

"If he's not stalking Kori than what the hell do you want to call it?"

"He can still be narcissistic and not a stalker right?"

Jonah shrugged his shoulder. "I suppose so."

"Narcissists believe they are above other people. Intellectually, physically, emotionally and probably spiritually though I'd guess the narcissist believes himself a god of some sort. It's possible all our suspects could harbor this idea of themselves."

"So what's your point Evan? This doesn't eliminate anyone."

"Maybe Kori isn't in as much immediate danger as we think. If getting her attention is what this guy is after, she'd really have to piss him off to fall out of favor with him. Maybe instead of sequestering Kori to her house we should be having her act a little bit more. Try and play into what he wants."

Jonah could see where Evan was going with this now but he still held his reservations. "Sounds like a good idea unless we're wrong. If we are dealing with a stalker we may just set him off."

"Well, so far, Kori sitting in her house or hiding out at the cafe hasn't stopped him from leaving notes or killing. Jonah, if I'm right, this guy wants her attention. He wants a positive view from her. He wants Kori to see him as he sees himself. If she keeps running he's going to get pissed which I think is why Boyd was murdered. Kori showed more attention to Boyd's presence in the cafe instead of looking around and trying to notice anybody else."

"So what do you want to do next?"

"Talk to Gabe Hathaway. And either today or tomorrow a visit to Matt McCleary would be nice. Except I'd like to approach these guy's a little differently. Let's see if we can get them to talk more about Kori and how they know her and relate to her. Maybe someone will stand out in their ravings."

"I think that before we talk to Hathaway we need to stop at Kori's. She's going to have a big part in this and I have a feeling she's not going to be extremely thrilled about this."

"Jonah I don't think playing the love interest to a killer is going to sound appealing to anyone."

"Probably not but let's go pitch the plan to Kori anyway."

Bakker and Harding arrived at Kori's house within a half-hour. Jonah noticed Elliot Bowman's car in the drive. Elliot looked as though a plague of frogs at his feet would have been more welcomed when he opened the door. A weary smile slid across Elliot's face. "My, my Detectives. We've seen each other twice in one day. What's the occasion? I've been interviewed already and formally tagged as a suspect in the terrorizing of my girlfriend. Have you finally come to charge me with murder?"

Jonah stood firmly and met Elliot's glare. "Professor Bowman, we have official business with Miss Chandler. That's why we came to her home and not yours. Now either let us in or go get her."

Elliot stepped back and let the detectives in. "Kori's resting upstairs. Give me a minute and I'll go get her."

Kori came downstairs with Elliot and Harley in tow. "What can I do for you Detectives?"

Jonah knew she was pissed. There was no pleasant greeting, no smile, and not even a first name. And she appeared to share Bowman's idea of a plague instead of seeing them. "I know you'd rather not deal with us right now but we need to speak with you alone. I promise we won't take much time."

"Detective, you may believe Elliot is responsible for my problems but I do not share that theory. If he wants to be with me he's more than welcome."

Elliot jumped in to stop the impending power struggle that was about to take place. "Actually I have some papers to go over if you don't mind?" Kori shook her head and said she'd be fine. She waited till he was upstairs before she turned her attention back to Detective Bakker. "Is it okay if I bring the dog with me?" Without waiting for an answer she led them into the kitchen. But as they entered the kitchen, Harley headed for the back door. Kori shook her head. Even the dog didn't want to be here.

"Would either of you like coffee or something else to drink?" They both said no and sat down at the table they'd occupied earlier. Kori grabbed a can of Coke from the refrigerator and sat down. "So what's the big news?"

Evan and Jonah decided on the ride over that Evan would do most of the talking. It wasn't so much that it was his idea but more that they figured Kori would be upset with Jonah for suspecting Elliot in the case. And from the look on Kori's face Evan was sure 'upset' was an understatement. "Kori, I don't necessarily believe we're looking so much for a stalker as someone who wants you for specific reasons known only to him."

"Isn't that a stalker?"

"I don't believe that's the case here. This guy seems to know you almost too well. Like he's been in your life before or still is and has decided he wants you all for himself. Unlike a typical stalking though, I think right now he simply wants to get your attention. Sort of like he's showing off his abilities."

"Well, he's definitely got my attention. I still don't see the difference Detective."

"I think you know this guy already. How well you know him remains to be seen. I believe Shelly Roberts was killed so you knew he existed. He may have tried to approach you before and felt he was unsuccessful and her murder would show you that you missed him. Boyd was probably murdered because the killer perceived Boyd as a viable threat to your attention."

"I barely spoke to Boyd that night."

"That's what we saw but not the killer."

Kori still wasn't sure what they were driving at exactly but she knew she was going to be part of the solution. "So what do you want me to do?"

Evan folded his hands on the table and leaned forward. "How well can you act?"

"I tried out for the school plays in high school every year. I never got a part. What do you want me to do?"

"Casually, start playing into this guy. If he wants your attention and amazement at his feats, than give it to him. Start commenting on the cleverness of the notes. How much you like Emily Dickinson and poetry in general. Maybe say something to the effect that Boyd never was really nice to you anyway."

Kori was shaking her head. "People are never going to believe me. Besides the fact that I'm going to look like a cold hearted bitch. I can't do that."

"We only want you to play to certain people."

"Like Elliot."

"Yes. And a couple others."

"Who exactly?"

"Gabe Hathaway."

Kori frowned and said, "Paige's handyman? I don't really know him. The most time I've spent with him is when he changed the locks on my doors."

"Whenever you get the chance with him. And how do you feel about Matt McCleary?"

"I think he's a real shit for what he's done to Paige. Are you suggesting he's behind this? That's stupid. Matt would barely notice me when I was around."

"Kori, please. Humor me then, and don't tell Paige or anyone else what you're doing—including Professor Bowman. Play up to his ego too for the sake of humoring me. And one more thing. Do you know anyone that may have kept in contact with Tyler Adams?"

"I told you before. When we divorced I cut all ties with him. That includes any mutual friends we had. And I'm not 'playing up' to Elliot. I won't lie to him."

"I didn't say lie."

"It's still lying by omission. And what ever happened to me staying in my house and never being left alone. Has that all changed too? Suddenly the guy wants to kill everyone but me?"

"Something like that. Like I've said Kori, I don't believe he wants to harm you. He wants you for some reason or another. Maybe having you will simply boost his ego. Who the hell knows. But caging you up isn't going to help if I'm right."

"And if you're wrong?"

Jonah finally spoke up. "We still don't want you alone. Even if we're wrong on this guy a police officer will still be around. Kori we are doing our best but in one week we have three dead bodies, four notes and shit to go on. You are the only link. Please just try and work with us on this.

"Lets say it turns out Elliot is the guy you want. Why go and tell him he's a suspect? I suppose you're planning on doing the same thing to Gabe Hathaway and Matt. Wouldn't it be easier to just let them be and think you're clueless, which apparently you are?"

Evan thought she was coming around to their idea so he took his time explaining anything she asked. "It would appear to be better to leave them alone but I don't want whomever it is to feel unthreatened. If we charge them as a suspect it may drive them on in their pursuit of you. If the guy feels too cocky he may drag this out for a while."

Kori tried to weigh the pros and cons of the situation quickly in her head. If she agreed to do this it may end sooner. If she decided they were nuts and didn't go along with them she could feel trapped for some time. Her life wasn't going to feel like her own until the guy was caught. But in the process of getting her life back she might destroy whatever relationship she had with Elliot. Not to mention Gabe would probably think she was a bitch for the way she talked about Boyd.

And what about Paige and Matt? Maybe Matt was having a midlife crisis and eventually they got back together. Would either of them forgive her for assuming Matt might be the one after her? There seemed to be more cons to this endeavor they wanted her to go on but none of the cons would really matter if she never had her life back. Or if this guy decided to kill another friend.

"Okay Detective Harding. I'll go along with this for a while. Though I'm not playing games for months. I want this over and I don't want anyone else to die because of me."

"Kori I promise we won't drag this out if we can help it." Harding looked like a walking contradiction. In some way it seemed a great weight had been lifted off his shoulders and at the same time another weight had been put on his back. Kori felt sorry for them in a way. She wouldn't want to be in their shoes with a killer on the loose, no clues and a temperamental victim.

She sighed, ran her fingers through her hair and got up from the table. "Is it alright if I go into work tomorrow?"

Jonah turned and looked at her. She was holding up better than he ever imagined she would and he was glad to see she was still determined to get on with life. "Go ahead into work but please don't go alone. Maybe keep Janine with you or have Miss McCleary sit with you. This guy might not want to hurt you but that's only a guess. I'd rather be safe than sorry. If you need a ride, let the officer outside know. Can you live with that?"

"Yeah. I've laid enough at Janine's feet though. I'll find someone to sit with me."

Jonah turned and walked out the door. Evan looked at Kori and gave a sympathetic smile. "I'm sorry for the way things are going Kori. And I'm sorry Bakker comes off as such a hard-ass but he's only trying to protect you. We both are. Thanks for working with us."

"I can see where Detective Bakker is coming from and I can see both of you are working hard at this. I don't mean to be difficult I just think your both wrong about Elliot."

"I hope we are too Kori. I'll talk to you later." With that he turned and walked out the door. Bakker had the car running and was ready to go. Kori wondered if Bakker really hoped it wasn't Elliot or that was just the polite thing for Harding to say. She closed the door and as she turned, saw Elliot and Harley coming from the kitchen.

Elliot smiled when he saw her standing at the door. "I heard a car start up and assumed it was safe to be near you. Any stunning revelations?"

She smiled and walked to the living room. "It's safe and nothing stunning ." She sat down on the couch and considered telling him what she and the detectives had talked about. Harley laid down at Kori's feet and Elliot sat next to her. Neither she nor Elliot said anything for a long time and the silence was beginning to strain Kori. He had to have known they talked about something important but he never asked and that was almost as unnerving as if he'd given her the third degree. She had to say something to him. "They asked me not to tell you what we talked about."

Elliot put his arm around her and pulled her closer to him. "I kind of guessed they would or I would have been invited to the conversation."

She closed her eyes so he wouldn't see the tears welling up in them. "I'm so sorry Elliot. For everything. I'm so afraid you'll get tired of this and just walk away."

"Kori I'm not going anywhere. I'm not the man they're looking for. I would never hurt you like this. And I care too much about you to just walk away. I've never walked away from anybody and I'm not going to start now."

They sat together for almost an hour without saying a word. He hadn't said he loved her but he did care for her. She thought that was a least some progress. During her worst time he was still with her. But despite his promise, Kori wondered how much he would take. She decided to let it be for now and just enjoy the moment she had now.

It was almost six o'clock and her mind started to wander to thoughts of work. Janine and Karen had been handling the opening and closing for most of the week and she really wanted to give them a break. "Do you have anything planned for the early morning?"

"Nope. My whole weekend is clear. I just figured I'd spend it with you."

"How would you feel about going to the cafe tonight? I'd like to give Janine a break if you don't mind sitting there with me?"

"I don't mind. Detective Bakker okayed you going to work?"

"Yep. As long as I wasn't alone he's fine with it."

"Let's go then."

While Kori and Elliot were making plans, Jonah and Evan had been parked outside Gabe Hathaway's condo. A half-hour of waiting finally paid off when they saw his red truck turn the corner and head straight towards their car. The detectives got out of the car at the same time Gabe was pulling in to his drive and they greeted him as he got out of the truck.

"Mr. Hathaway? Detective Bakker. Mind if we talk for a minute?"

"Not at all Detective. Come on in."

The three men walked to the condo together. Upon entering, Evan and Jonah had the same impression. A bachelor's pad if they'd ever seen one. They came in through the kitchen, which held the essentials found in every kitchen and a small wood table with two chairs. The living room was just barely visible and all they could see was a couch, a rocking chair, a coffee table and one end table. Jonah wondered if there was more in there they couldn't see but doubted it. He also doubted they'd be invited to see it after they talked with Gabe.

"I've got another job to be at in an hour so what is it that I can help you with?"

"Do you happen to know a man named Tyler Adams?"

Gabe thought for a second and shook his head. "Not that I know of. Should I?"

"Not necessarily. Just thought I'd ask. You do work for Paige and Matt McCleary don't you?"

"Yes. That's where I'm headed when we're through here. I'm starting on the kitchen remodeling. Why?"

"Do you know Mr. McCleary well?"

"Nope. Never met him. Paige always asked that I start after he left for work and finish before he got home."

"Is that odd for you or have you had other requests like that?"

"One other client I worked for made basically the same arrangement. Her husband worked nights and needed to sleep during the day so I worked nights while he was gone."

Jonah paused for a moment and watched Gabe. If he was trying to hide anything he was very good at it. His facial expression gave nothing away. He'd bet Gabe did well playing poker. "Do you know Kori Chandler well?"

"I wouldn't say, "Well". Paige has talked about her and I know what she's going through but besides changing her locks I don't think I've ever really spoke to her. Oh, and the night we were all at the cafe I talked to her a bit but that's about it."

"Have you heard about Boyd Thomas?"

"I'd have to live in a bubble to not have."

"Where were you between four and seven this morning?"

"Sleeping until six. Then I got up and went jogging."

"Where do you jog?"

"Around the lake to downtown and then back."

"Mr. Hathaway we're here to tell you that you are now officially a suspect in the murders of Michelle Roberts and Boyd Thomas. Anyone who could verify your whereabouts this morning?"

"Kind of strange being a suspect, seeing that I don't even really know Kori Chandler. But as far as my whereabouts go, Janine opened Kori's Cafe early and I stopped for coffee. Must have been around six thirty."

"We'll check with Janine then. Not planning on leaving town anytime soon are you?"

"Hadn't planned on it."

"Well let's just keep it that way then shall we? We won't take up anymore of your time. Thank you Mr. Hathaway."

"Any time Detectives'."

Gabe watched them go, closed the door and headed for the shower. Normally he wouldn't bother to shower in between jobs but then Paige was different. He might work in her kitchen for a while though he'd bet he'd work harder in her bedroom. The detectives were asking a lot about Matt, and Gabe figured that meant Matt was out as a husband, and in as a suspect.

It still seemed odd they chose him as a suspect since he barely knew Kori and that must mean they're grasping at straws. He stripped off his clothes and turned on the water as hot as he could stand it. He supposed most men would kill to be in bed with Paige and it wasn't that he was complaining either. Paige was gorgeous but she just wasn't quite his type. He preferred the quiet ones. Ones like Kori Chandler.

Gabe finished showering and dried off. His bedroom was as sparsely furnished as the rest of the place. A bed on a metal frame, a dresser and a nightstand. The only things that could be considered decorations were a mirror on the closet door, two dark blue mini-blinds over the windows and a few picture frames. He pulled on a clean pair of jeans, a gray sweatshirt and his work boots. He put on some cologne and grabbed his wallet.

Paige had called earlier and asked him to come by and talk about the remodeling of the kitchen. He wondered if she cooked because so far all she'd fed him was pizza. He decided to make himself a sandwich before heading over there. He wanted to feel bad about sleeping with Paige, while really wanting someone like Kori, but always managed to talk himself out of the guilt.

He didn't believe he was Paige's type of guy either. She'd been hurt by her husband's cheating and he was simply in the right spot when she went on the rebound. Gabe was halfway through his dinner when the phone rang.

"Hello?'

"Hi. It's me, Paige. I figured you'd be here by now."

"Sorry but I got held up a bit."

"Nothing serious I hope?"

"No. I'm just about ready to walk out the door."

"Have you eaten yet?"

"You going to cook for me?"

"I'll supply the steaks if you grill'em."

"I think I can handle that. I'll see you in about fifteen minutes."

"Okay. Bye."

Gabe looked down at the half of sandwich he still held in his hand. "Guess I can throw you out." He pitched the sandwich and got his car keys. He smiled to himself thinking maybe she'd cook if she knew how. He wondered if he should tell her he's now a suspect in the murders and was still debating the issue when he arrived at her house. He sat in his truck for a minute and decided if she asked again what held him up, he'd tell her about the detectives. Otherwise, he didn't see what business it was of hers anyway.

He got out of the truck and headed toward the back door. Maybe he could get around to asking Paige if she knew when Kori would be back to work. Gabe saw a gas grill sitting on the back porch. He went to the door, knocked, and let himself in. Paige was standing at the sink cutting up carrots to add to a bowl of salad. She had on a oversized sweatshirt that hung to her thighs and spandex bike shorts. Her blonde hair was pulled back into a ponytail and she looked like she was just old enough to vote.

"Hi. Hope you like salad. I'd make the steaks but if you like your steak any other way than well done, you'd better do it yourself."

Gabe laughed. "I'll man the grill. How do you like yours done?"

"A little pink inside but I don't want it to moo when I stick the knife in."

"I think I can handle that." Paige handed him the plate with the steaks on it. "Be back in few minutes."

Paige was not an overly emotional woman but she stood at the sink and struggled to hold back the tears. She tried not to think about Matt or how many times they had shared an evening just like this one. She realized she would never have one of those nights with Matt again. She wanted to pick up the phone and call him but she didn't even have his new number. And then what would she say anyway? *How's your new girlfriend? I'm having dinner with my handyman. Oh, by the way, sorry I mentioned your name as a possible suspect in the stalking and murder case.*

Maybe she should call Kori. She had to be losing her mind. But like Kori didn't have enough problems. Besides, Kori couldn't even figure out what was going on with Elliot much less sort out Gabe and Matt. She had to shake this line of thought away. Matt was gone and outside her house stood a handsome young man who she hoped could cook as well as he made love. Paige was determined to have a wonderful night. She'd call and check on Kori in the morning and then she'd call Detective Harding and see if they'd made any headway with Matt or anyone else.

Gabe walked in and thought for a second Paige looked ready to cry but decided it had to be the light in the kitchen. "Steaks are ready and I promise you won't think you're eating on a farm." She gave a weak smile and now he wondered if his first impression of Paige near tears was right. The idea of Paige being miserable had never really crossed his mind before this moment but he took a step back and tried to see Paige with a different eye.

"Paige are you all right?"

She felt worse because she could hear genuine concern in his voice. She wanted this to be a wonderful evening of good food, good conversation and great sex. What was about to happen would turn this into a pity party thrown by herself for herself. The food would be tasteless and he'd end up going home depressed after listening to her sob story. If she was smart, she'd put a rush on the remodeling before they both ended up on Prozac. "I'm fine." That sounded safe. "Let's eat. The steaks smell great and look better than my charred version."

"Paige if you'd rather wait for another evening to go over the kitchen plans its no problem."

"No really it's fine. Gives my mind something to ponder."

They spent the next hour and a half eating and going over the new kitchen plans. He wanted to put ceramic tile on the floor and an island to add more counter space. They talked of moving counters from one side of the kitchen to the other and freeing up space to put in a sliding glass door out to the porch. Colors for walls, floors and counters were tossed around and she promised she'd stop and get color samples from the hardware store.

The conversation had stalled and for a while they sat and looked at each other. Paige smiled softly and asked, "So how was the rest of your day?"

"Not bad. A patch job here, a closet organizer there. Not much to it."

"What tied you up earlier?"

"Are you sure you want to know?"

"Did you ever notice how often you answer a question with a question? As long as it wasn't another woman you were with, yes, I'd like to know."

"Bakker and Harding stopped by my place. Asked me a few questions and then told me I was officially a suspect in the murders that have taken place. I guess that includes being the author of the mysterious notes also."

"Oh god Gabe! I'm so sorry! What a couple of assholes. You don't even know Kori do you?"

"No. Like I told them, the most I ever talked to her was when I changed the locks on her doors. Doesn't really matter. I'm not a killer and I'm not harassing Kori either. Eventually they'll figure that out."

Paige was beginning to see Kori's plight in life. The one man she wanted to be with was now a murder suspect and there wasn't a damn thing she could do about it. It must be driving Kori crazy to know the police suspect Elliot. Paige looked at Gabe and knew no matter what he had told her, he was bothered being seen as a suspect. She had the incredible urge to wrap her arms around him but stayed where she was. It took her a minute to realize that if she wanted to hug him she could. Matt wasn't coming back to her. Now it was a matter of technicalities like divorce papers.

She got up from her chair and stood in front of Gabe. Slowly, she tipped forward and wrapped her arms around his neck. Paige positioned her mouth right next to his ear. Softly she whispered, "I'm sorry if knowing me is bringing you trouble." And gently she kissed his neck. She felt his hands come up and cover hers. Paige thought he'd stop there but his hands kept moving up. Gabe ran his hands up her arms and neck until he'd placed a hand on each side of her head. He turned his head and gently tilted her head until they were face to face.

He caressed her cheeks and lips with light kisses till he couldn't wait any longer. He pushed his chair back and at the same time guided Paige so that she was standing in front of him. Gabe stared at her for a moment and then slid his hands up the front of her shirt. As his hands went forward, Gabe stood up. In one swift movement Paige's sweatshirt was over her head and off her body. She hadn't bothered to put a bra on which just let him view her incredible body all the faster.

Gabe pulled his sweatshirt off and slid his fingers around the waist of Paige's shorts and pulled down. He followed them down her thighs until he was sure the shorts would slide the rest of the way off. Paige had begun working on unbuttoning his jeans. She started unzipping them and whispered into Gabe's ear, "Take me upstairs."

He stepped back and looked at her intense brown eyes. He reached behind her and shoved the dinner dishes halfway across the table, put his hands around her waist, picked her up and set her on the table. "I think right here is just fine." She never had the chance to respond back because in an instant his mouth was covering hers. Her breath caught as he forcefully plunged his tongue in and out a few times then slowed down and expertly glided it back and forth over hers.

Paige used her feet to push his jeans down to his knees and then wrapped her legs around his waist. The gentleness he'd used a few days ago was tonight replaced by hunger she'd never really experienced. He'd taken her like he'd kissed her. Forcefully, then slow and rhythmic. She moaned quietly and leaned back on her hands enjoying the pleasure he was bringing her. It seemed to last forever until that moment came when it felt as if an electrical current flowed through every nerve and her whole body shook with an intensity unknown before now.

She sat forward and slumped into Gabe's arms. He chuckled softly as he kissed her neck up and down. "Never had it on the kitchen table did you?"

"Can't say that I have. You know this is going to cost me a new table don't you?"

"Why?" He continued to kiss her neck as they quietly talked to each other.

"I honestly don't think I could invite my parents up from Arizona to eat on this table."

He looked at her and when he saw she was serious he had to laugh. "Paige, I figured you for being outrageous enough to do something like this! I can't believe you'd actually ditch this table now."

"Fond memories or not I just couldn't do it."

Gabe pulled away from her and pulled up his pants. He found his sweatshirt and put it on. "I hate to run out on you but I have an early start tomorrow morning." He'd found her shirt and handed it to her.

Paige put on her clothes and looked at him. She knew this was nothing but a fling but she was starting to feel cheap. Early morning or not, he could make an effort to stay longer. But she knew better than to push the subject. That would only drive him away faster. And until she found her footing again in life it was her opinion that this was better than nothing at all. "Do you feel like trying to start this kitchen on Monday?" That would give him two days of breathing room.

"Monday's fine. I'll try and stop by tomorrow though and see what colors you're looking at for floors. Maybe I can get some ceramic tiles for you to choose from while I start tearing this floor out."

"Sounds good. I'll probably be at Kori's sometime. Just give me a call."

He pulled on his jacket and walked over to Paige. He kissed her so softly this time it reminded her of Matt. "See ya tomorrow." He walked out the door without a glance back. Just as Matt had done the evening she confronted him. Sometimes she wondered if getting involved with Gabe was a good idea or one of the more stupid things she'd done in life. "Oh well. What's done is done. I might as well enjoy it while it lasts."

She picked up the phone and dialed Kori's number. She gave up on the sixth ring. Paige, on her way to bed, wondered if Kori had finally gotten Elliot into bed. If she hadn't, Kori better have a good explanation why she isn't home like the detectives told her.

Kori and Elliot were still in the cafe at ten o'clock. She could have closed it at nine but nobody was stopping in anyway and her work was getting done. Janine had been both worried and excited to see her come in. It took Kori twenty minutes to assure Janine it was fine if she left for the night. Kori explained that Elliot would sit while Kori worked and then take her home. Kori would also open in the morning so Janine could sleep in one day.

Janine thanked her for the hundredth time and finally headed out the door. Elliot sat quietly through the entire conversation but had his say after Janine left. "She acts like she finally found a boyfriend?"

Kori eyed him warily. "And you're the official on how women look when they're in love?"

"No I'm not the official or an expert on the matter. I've just never seen a woman get that excited over a girl's night out or a ride home. So you're telling me you never got giddy or goofy before a date with me?"

Smiling, Kori said, "I don't think I've ever gotten 'giddy' over anything. Goofy a time or two but not over a guy."

"So how did you feel when we started dating?"

"The same way I feel now when I see you, excited."

"Oh that was good Kori." He smiled. Kori loved that smile and felt like she hadn't seen it in ages. There was nothing behind it like sympathy or worry, just a genuine smile. She liked being with him and if nothing else, this nightmare she was living was giving her more time with him.

"Why don't we call it a night? I told Janine I'd open in the morning so if you don't mind sitting with me in the morning until I get a hold of Paige, I'd appreciate it."

"I don't mind spending time with you. Besides, whenever Paige rolls out of bed and gets here, I'll just shoot over to my office for a while and get some work done for Monday."

Kori hit the switches that turned out the lights and they walked out together and went back to her house. Elliot slept on the couch and after Kori had gotten him settled she went up to her room. They were moving at a snails pace but she was getting used to it now. As she slipped beneath the covers of her bed she thought about what Detectives' Bakker and Harding had said and what she knew they believed. And then she thought of the man sleeping on her couch right below her. Kori prayed she was right about Elliot and he was the man she believed him to be.

CHAPTER 8

The next two weeks went as normal as life had been before Kori found Shelly Roberts in her back yard. Kori and Elliot attended Boyd's wake and funeral the Monday following his death. Half the town was there because they either knew Boyd or were part of the curious crowd. Nothing had really changed between Kori and Elliot either and he continued to sleep on her couch.

Work hours returned to the norm also. Kori went to the cafe in the late afternoon with Paige and Elliot would meet there at dinner time and replace Paige. Paige was spending more time in the bookstore and was driving the manager of the place crazy. Paige still saw Gabe and they continued to remodel the house little by little but she never mentioned that she was sleeping with Gabe to Kori again. Kori never asked and since Paige never brought it up.

Detectives Bakker and Harding had gone to the accounting firm where Matt worked, only to be told he had taken an extended vacation and wouldn't return for two weeks. No bodies had turned up and Kori hadn't received any more notes or phone calls. Everything appeared to be settling down and Kori was beginning to relax a bit more. The only ones who were still worried were the detectives.

Tuesday morning jolted Kori back into the real world as sure as if someone had put a firecracker in her kitchen. Kori couldn't see why Paige had to continue to come over every morning. After two weeks with no further threats, even Bakker couldn't justify the expense of an around-the-clock cruiser to the department. It was a beautiful day and the perfect October morning with the air cool and crisp and a slight breeze coming from the north.

Kori had gotten up early and by seven thirty was working on her second cup of coffee. Harley had been laying on the rug by the kitchen sink when Kori had the idea of taking Harley for a walk. "How about a walk this morning, boy?" Harley lifted his head and perked his ears. She couldn't remember the last time she'd been this awake and this motivated so early. A quiet walk might do them both wonders. "Give me five minutes to do something with my hair and attire and maybe we'll head down by the lake. How's that sound? And if we're both feeling up to it maybe we'll go get Paige this morning." Harley was up and moving toward the stairs. Obviously he liked her as a morning person.

Five minutes turned into fifteen when Kori finally looked in the mirror. It had been easier to just tie her hair back and slip on a baseball cap than actually fix it. The two slipped out the back door to avoid a police escort. Though she hated the idea of going anywhere near the tree that once held Shelly Roberts body, she desperately wanted to feel normal again. To feel that, required her to leave the police sitting in front of her house.

As they walked together in the relative quiet, Kori realized how much she'd missed having time to herself. She enjoyed having Elliot around and even Paige but sometimes she just liked being alone. The police were no closer to solving the two murders than they were after they happened, but Kori had done as the detectives asked.

She still refused to act out the scenario that Bakker had wanted her to for Elliot but she did her best with Gabe whenever she saw him. Matt hadn't been around so she didn't have to worry about him. She did worry what that did to Paige though. Kori had seen Paige with Gabe enough to know they had something going on and guessed she was still sleeping with him, but that really wasn't any of Kori's business. Paige knew from Detective Harding that Matt was on vacation and she knew Paige assumed he was with his new love. Why the detective was telling Paige Matt's whereabouts she had no idea and didn't want to know.

Kori and Harley reached the lake and she was even happier that they'd ventured out. The leaves had already turned and most had fallen but the area was still beautiful in the morning sun. They passed one couple and two joggers but for now only they were on the path. She sat on a bench overlooking the lake soaking up the quiet of the day and was about to start back when she heard the soft slapping of jogging feet slow down and stop a few feet away from her. She turned and saw Gabe Hathaway approaching her and Harley.

"Morning Kori. Out by yourself for a change, eh?"

"We felt kind of daring today. Don't you work today?" Kori had let go of Harley's leash so he could sniff away at a tree he found very intriguing.

"I'm spending the day at Paige's. All that's left in the kitchen is to put in the new countertops so I opted to schedule the whole day for that. Probably won't take that but maybe we can start on something else then."

"How much could possibly be left?"

"Haven't you seen the place lately?"

"Paige won't let me in till you two are through. It must be good because I don't think I've ever seen Paige get excited over decorating."

"Not much is left and the house does look a lot different. The kitchen turned out better than I'd even hoped for. So where are the two of you headed next?"

"We were going to stop by Paige's but I'm guessing she'll be over later if you're going over there. We'll just go home now and I'll call her."

"She strikes me as the mother hen when it comes to you. Better hope she don't call while you're gone."

"Even if she calls I'm already out. I'll just get another lecture like I did a couple of weeks ago when she didn't know where I was."

"You know, I don't think I've seen you since Boyd's funeral. How you doing? You look good. Rested at the least."

Kori heard the door of opportunity open and it was Bakker's voice beckoning her in. "I'm fine. Boyd and I weren't all that close anymore."

"You two were together for a while though right?"

Her smile tightened a bit and she swallowed hard but continued the charade anyway. "Boyd was a part of my past and it's always difficult to let go but he wasn't that special to me. If he was we'd still be together." She felt like a complete idiot. Even if Boyd wasn't the love of her life he'd been there for her. Four, mostly wonderful, years and now she stood in front of a nearly total stranger making it appear Boyd was the problem. And Gabe was standing there staring at her.

"Well, I can kind of grasp your point. I am really glad you're doing okay. Paige has been worried about you."

"Tell her to stop worrying. I really am fine."

"Paige won't listen but I'll tell her. I better take off. I'll catch you later Kori."

"Bye Gabe." Kori stood where she was feeling the freshness of the day draining from her. Harley was onto the next tree and she called for him. "Come on boy. It's not even nine yet and I've made a complete ass of myself. That's got to be a new record for me."

Whatever vigor she had felt at seven thirty was now gone. Lying to people so early in the morning must drag her down. Harley must have sensed the shift in her mood because even he seemed to be shuffling along a bit.

As they turned the corner of their street, Kori could see a car parked in her drive. Even as they got closer she still couldn't recognize who it belonged to. "Looks like we have a visitor Harley. Now we just have to figure out if that's good or bad." Kori hesitated a moment as she reached her drive. She'd planned on going in the back door but now considered the front in case she needed to run.

Just then a man walked from around the side of the house. She recognized him as soon as he came into clear view. But Kori didn't know if she should breath yet or not. A visit from Matt McCleary probably wasn't going to be a good thing.

"Morning Kori. It's been a while. How've you been lately?"

He looked as he always had. In a way this surprised her. She was expecting to see a difference in him. Something that would tell her the man she'd know for over a decade would never leave her best friend the way he did. "I've been all right. What can I do for you?"

Matt didn't speak right away and Kori could feel her adrenaline kick in. She wanted to run but to where she didn't know. Harley stood next to her and she knew if she ran for the house he'd follow but something in the back of her mind told her stay where she was. If they stayed in the drive at least they were in the open.

He cleared his throat and said, "I'd just like a minute of your time. I got home from vacation to find half a dozen messages for me to contact the police in Tabor. I went to the police station Monday and talked to Detective Bakker but I'm still a little confused. I thought maybe you could clear some things up for me."

"If you're confused about something I think the police would be your best bet for clarification Matt." She could see his jaw clenching and guessed that wasn't the answer he was looking for.

"Kori we've been friends for what? Twelve or Thirteen years? You can't give me five minutes?"

She wondered why she didn't just stay in bed. How many beautiful fall days had she missed in her life? And today of all days she decides this one can't slip away. Kori tried to speak as slowly as she could so he would believe she wasn't afraid of him. "The man I've been friends with for over a decade doesn't exist anymore. The man I knew would never have done what you did to Paige. Whatever issues the police have with you I am not privy too. So, no Matt, I don't have five minutes for you."

Kori knew with those words she'd really pissed him off. His face was becoming tinged with red and his hands curled into fists. She continued to watch him work his jaw muscles and wished someone would interrupt them soon. Then she noticed the low growl coming from Harley and looked down to see the hair standing up on his back. Kori wasn't sure what Harley was capable of but if Matt came any closer she decided she would let go of his leash and find out.

Through clenched teeth Matt said, "You have no idea what it was like. Paige is a spoiled, privileged bitch. She thinks if she wants it then she deserves it."

At first Kori couldn't understand why he stopped talking and then she heard footsteps behind her. She was too scared to turn around but she was never so happy to hear Detective Bakker's voice in all her life. "Mr. McCleary." He looked from McCleary to Kori. As his gazed went back to Matt, he said, "This probably isn't a good idea to be here." He walked in front of Kori blocking her view of Matt.

"We're old friends. I didn't think it was against the law to visit old friends."

"From the look of things, I'd say Miss Chandler doesn't consider you a friend any longer. And under the circumstances I would think you'd know better Mr. McCleary. So I'm asking you to leave now."

It seemed more like hours than seconds before she saw Matt walk over to his car and get in. He hit the gas so hard she thought he'd fly into the yard across the street but he stayed on the road and off he went. Kori almost felt relieved until she looked at Detective Bakker's face and knew she had a new anger to deal with.

"And just what in hell do you think you're doing? I thought I told you I didn't want you alone?"

"It was just a walk."

"And what if a police officer hadn't spotted you in the park? A car only drives by every half hour Kori. From the look of things, the killer could have grabbed you, threw you in his car and nobody would have known."

"I'm sorry. Things have seemed so normal lately."

"That's what this guy wants. He's waiting for you to feel secure again Kori. He wants to strike when you least expect it. Let's go in."

It was like being woken up abruptly. Kori wasn't sure what had just happened and it took her a while to fully grasp the situation. Kori and Bakker went in to the kitchen and she put on a pot of coffee. Bakker hadn't said another word to her and she knew he was furious. She guessed if she were in his shoes she'd feel the same way. "Jonah I really am sorry."

"Being sorry could have killed you. What if Matt is the nut running around?"

"Are you married?"

"What?"

"I asked you if you were married."

He stood by the door and didn't say anything at first.

"It's not a difficult question Bakker."

"Never said it was. I was just trying to figure out why you'd want to know. Yes, I'm married."

"Do you think your wife could be with you and one other person for weeks and not want to escape at some point?"

"Kori I didn't say I couldn't understand why you went out. I'm just asking for a little more time. I realize this must be very frustrating for you but we are in the same boat."

"No we're not in the same boat. Your life isn't in question every time you step outside because someone happens to think you're the only one for him."

"I'm just the one that's got to catch the son of bitch that wants you because he thinks you're the one for him. Same boat Kori. You're just sitting on a different end than I am."

Kori finally woke up and was able to clearly understand where she was and what was on the line. No matter how frustrating life seemed it could get worse. She felt horrible for being such a pain in the ass and giving Bakker grief over him doing his job.

"Kori you didn't happen to sell Matt on the idea that the murders didn't really bother you by chance?"

"No. Sorry. I was busy being a little paranoid at the time. But I did mention the idea to Gabe earlier."

"When did you see him?"

"Harley and I were in the park and he was jogging. We only talked briefly though."

"I don't suppose you've said anything to Bowman have you?"

"No. I can't do that Jonah. I won't say what you and I talk about but I won't lie to Elliot. Elliot has been around long enough to know how things effect me. Same thing applies to Matt." Kori stopped talking abruptly as a new thought hit her. Matt tore out of her drive like he was on some kind of mission. Kori had the feeling his mission was to go straight to Paige. Bakker was watching and waiting for her to say something when the phone rang. She picked up the receiver, still occupied with the idea that Matt was probably headed to Paige's.

"Hello?" There was no response. Again she said, "Hello?" She looked over at the Caller ID to see 'unknown' displayed in the little window. Kori turned to Bakker to tell him but he was already getting up from his seat when she heard the familiar whisper of her name. "Who is this?" In the quiet she heard her tormenter whisper, "Have a nice walk Kori?" As Bakker reached her she heard the distinct click of the other line disconnecting and then the faint humming of an open line.

Bakker took the phone from her, listened for a second and replaced the phone. He looked at Kori and asked what happened.

"Same guy that called. Whispered to me again. I can't place the voice." She sat down hard on the kitchen chair. "He asked if I had a nice walk." Jonah could feel the anger rising up inside of him. Not only because he was angry at himself for not catching the guy yet but for what he was doing to Kori. For the first time that he could remember in his police career he felt his heart ache as she looked up at him with tears in her eyes and said, "He's still watching me."

Jonah picked up the phone, dialed quickly and waited for an answer. "Evan? Do me a favor. Without making this widely known, get a couple of guys together and find out where Bowman, Hathaway and Matt McCleary are right now."

Hearing Matt's name mentioned reminded Kori what she was going to tell Bakker before the phone call. "Jonah I think Matt was going to Paige's house when he left here."

"Evan I want you to go to McCleary's house. Matt may have gone there. Send someone else to the college and another cop to find Hathaway. If Hathaway's not found in twenty minutes put out an APB on his truck."

He hung up the phone and turned to Kori. She sat at the table with her face in her hands. She wasn't crying as far as he could tell but if she did Jonah wouldn't blame her. A person could only take so much before the pressure built enough to cave him or her in. Jonah walked over to Kori and put his hand on her shoulder. "I promise you Kori, we're going to get him soon." He hoped it wasn't an empty promise.

Evan sent two officers to the college and two separate cruisers out to find Gabe Hathaway. He told them to note where the two men were and meet at Kori Chandlers' house. He made it to Paige's house in seven minutes and noticed the dark green Chevy in the drive. He parked on the street and walked to the back of the house. As he got to the back door, Evan could hear drawers slamming from somewhere in the house. He saw Paige sitting at the kitchen table obviously upset and crying. Her whole body was shaking. Evan knocked and opened the door as Paige lifted her head. Immediately he saw the red imprint of a hand on the side of her face.

"Where's Matt?"

Paige put her head down again and talked to the floor. "He's upstairs getting his things. If you leave him alone he'll be gone soon."

"Has he been here long?"

"About fifteen minutes."

Evan ignored Paige's request to leave him alone and headed upstairs. Matt was still in the master bedroom when Evan found him. "Packing for good I hope."

Matt whirled around to see who had spoken. "Who the fuck are you?"

Harding paused a second before answering him. "Detective Harding."

Through clenched teeth, Matt hissed, "This is my house. I can take whatever belongs to me. You got a problem with that too?"

"I have a problem with assault. How long have you been here?"

"And that concerns you how?"

"How long have you been here Mr. McCleary? We can do this here or at the station."

Matt rolled his eyes. "Twenty minutes, tops. I've been up here packing for about ten minutes. Is that enough for you?"

Evan didn't bother answering his question. "Are you planning on going back to Newton Falls?"

"That's where I live now."

"You didn't answer the question."

"Yes. I'm going back to my home in Newton Falls. May I go now?"

"Not planning any more long vacations are you?"

"No. I think I'll save up for a lawyer just in case you plan on harassing me."

"No harassing here. Just don't leave Newton Falls. You're officially a suspect in the murders of Shelly Roberts and Boyd Thomas."

"You people really are desperate aren't you?"

"And I think I'll explain to Paige her right to press charges against you for assault."

"Go ahead Detective. You know where to reach me." Matt grabbed a couple of duffel bags and headed out the door.

Evan got his radio and spoke very slowly into it. "Jonah? You read me?"

"I read you. Go ahead."

"I have Matt here at Paige's house. What exactly are you looking for?"

"Has he been alone at any time in the last half hour?"

"Five maybe ten minutes. He's leaving now. Want me to detain him?"

"Not yet. Find out from Paige just exactly when he was alone and for how long."

"Got it. I should be with you shortly."

Evan walked back downstairs to the kitchen. Paige was still sitting at the table but had regained some of her composure. The mark Matt had left with his hand on her face wasn't quite as red as when he'd walked in. He stood next to her and gently asked if he could talk with her a minute. She nodded yes and he sat down across from her at the table.

"Want to tell me what happened?"

She looked everywhere but at his eyes and knew she must be embarrassed. "I heard him pull in and he walked in here screaming at me. Yelling at me that I must be quite bitter to sic the police on him or have my friend do it, for a murder he had nothing to do with. I told him I didn't know him anymore and he seemed so good at lying lately what else should I expect. I said it was me that suggested the police look in to his whereabouts and that Kori never said a word about him. That's when he slapped me. Called me a few names and said he was going to go up and pack his clothes. He would have his lawyers contact me and that I would never have to see him again."

Evan saw fresh tears in her eyes and wanted to tell her she'd be okay but he couldn't promise something he wasn't certain about. He went on questioning her. "Can you say how long he was alone upstairs before I got here?"

Paige was staring at the table and for a moment he thought she hadn't heard him. Evan was about to repeat the question when she answered. "Not longer than ten minutes. Could have been more or less but not by much. Why is that so important to you?"

"Detective Bakker wants to know."

"And where is he?"

Evan thought about not telling her but he figured she'd find out from Kori soon enough. "He's with Kori at her home."

Paige looked up and this time she had no problem looking him in the eye. "Has something happened to Kori?"

"I'm not sure exactly what's going on. Bakker called me on my cell phone and wanted a low profile on what he wanted me to do. He never said why. I'm headed over there now."

"I'd like to come with you. If you don't want to take me I'll drive myself."

Evan knew she would get there one way or another so he said she could ride with him.

Evan and Paige arrived at Kori's about fifteen minutes later. Paige sat straighter in her seat when she saw a police cruiser in the drive but Evan said he expected one to be there and possibly two more. She looked at him but never questioned why police cars were gathering at her friends' house. They walked up the path to the front door and Paige let herself in. They ran into the officer Evan had sent to the college, in the hall leading to the kitchen. He told them he'd filled in Bakker on what he'd found and continued on his way out.

Paige entered the kitchen and eyed Kori. They remained that way for a minute or two and then both nervously laughed. Paige walked over to Kori shaking her head. They hugged each other and Evan heard Paige say, "What a fucked up morning. What happened to you and what's with the cavalry?"

They let go of each other and Kori began briefing Paige on the events of the last few hours. "I was up early so Harley and I decided to take a walk."

"By yourself?"

"No. I wasn't alone. I had Harley. Besides it didn't get really bad till I got home and found Matt in my drive. Jonah showed up in time to save the day. We were in here talking and I was about to suggest someone go check on you when the phone rang."

"Your admirer I suppose?"

"Yeah. Implied he watched me walking this morning."

"Kori are you stupid or just trying to get killed?"

"Neither. It was nice out and I was trying to pretend life was normal."

Bakker spoke up at that point saying, "And now we know life is not normal yet. No more outings for Kori, right?"

"No but I'm not putting up with this much longer Jonah."

Paige wrinkled her brow and was shaking her head. "I'm still a little confused. If Harding came to my house looking for Matt then what are the other cops looking for?"

Kori answered her. "Elliot and Gabe. They want to see where those two were and where Matt was when the call came through."

"This guy whispers to you right?"

"Yeah. That's why I can't place the voice. Sometimes I think I should know it but I don't."

Paige sat down and looked at Evan. "Listen, I know I sent you after Matt but if the guy on the phone was whispering and calm about the matter then it couldn't have been Matt. Quiet and calm are two words I'd never use to describe our encounter and I doubt he'd have cooled off much going upstairs. Did they find Elliot or Gabe?"

Evan could see her point about Matt but he refused to rule out any possibility. He turned to Jonah but he simply shrugged his shoulders. "People can surprise you all the time. I'm not ready to say it was impossible for him to make the call." Evan looked back to Jonah. "What did they find out about the other two?"

Bakker sighed. "Bowman says he stepped out of his office for approximately forty-five minutes to help a study group but can't say with certainty what time that took place and none of the kids located from the group can say what time Bowman arrived. As for Gabe, we don't know yet. Haven't seen him but he may be at a job."

Paige frowned. "I thought he was supposed to be doing some work at the diner across from the college. But I'm not sure when that was supposed to happen. It was a one-day thing. Something with fixing a leaky roof or replacing wiring. Something like that."

Every one in the room focused on Paige. Kori wondered if something was still going on with the two of them and now she knew. Most employers don't know about their contractors upcoming work. Sounded more like 'pillow talk' to Kori but she held out hope she was wrong. If Paige was mixed up with Gabe on a personal level then she was most likely 'on the rebound' and those relationships never work out. Evan and Jonah looked at her curiously but didn't say a word.

The arrival of a police officer broke the silence in the kitchen. He came in the house and informed Bakker that they did indeed find Gabe working at the diner. Gabe said he never left the attic where he was repairing wires and nobody noticed that he'd left at any time. Bakker and Harding took their leave shortly after the officer left.

Kori and Harley walked them to the door and she thought she'd get them out of the house without another lecture from Bakker but she was wrong. Kori decided this was her day to be wrong about everything so why stop now.

"Kori I want someone with you at all times. You understand what I'm saying?"

"Yes."

"And I mean it. I don't want you alone in the morning, noon or evening. Not in the house, at work, when you're sleeping, never." Bakker felt as though he was sounding like her father but if it kept her safe he didn't care.

"Yes, I understand Detective. Not in a house, not with mouse, not with a fox, not in a box. I get it." Kori smiled as Bakker shook his head.

"Great. I got a killer quoting Emily Dickinson and the target of the killer is quoting me Dr. Seuss. I'll keep in touch." He walked to the car continuing to shake his head. Maybe Bakker really was the Cat in the Hat. He comes in to solve her problem, makes a bigger mess then her, cleans it up and then leaves. Maybe it was almost over. Life was quite a mess so he should be nearing the end were he cleans it all up. If he is "The Cat in the Hat".

Kori went back to the kitchen to find Paige drinking a cup of coffee. Kori reached on top of the refrigerator and grabbed a pack of cigarettes. She took one out and lit it. Exhaling deeply Kori sat across from Paige, lost in her own thoughts. Paige took a sip of coffee and cleared her throat.

"Well I guess this makes it official."

Kori looked up at Paige. "Makes what official?"

"You've had a really bad day if you're smoking."

"And just exactly when was the last time you settled for a normal cup of coffee? Since I opened the cafe? Your day has been just as shitty as mine has. And what's the mark on your face?"

"I finally pissed Matt off enough."

Kori's jaw dropped open. "He actually hit you?"

"Yeah, Matt's just full of surprises lately."

They sat together quietly for some time before Kori couldn't take it any longer. "I need to go to work. I still can't just sit here. It's like saying he's won the game. Let me get ready and we'll be out of here in half an hour." She finished her cigarette and headed upstairs.

Paige waited patiently, drinking her coffee and thinking. She thought about the day she confronted Matt about his mother and how cold he was. If he could be like that, was it possible he could turn his emotions on and off enough to make the phone call from upstairs? Paige doubted it but she still wasn't sure. It was going on noon and it had been a hell of a day so far. Paige kept going back to the same thought though. The past two weeks had been calm. Almost too calm in retrospect. Was today the beginning of the storm? If it was, she was afraid it would reach hurricane force proportions and she wondered who would be left standing in the end.

Kori and Paige reached the cafe at ten minutes till one and the 'lunch bunch' were starting to leave. Janine was busy cleaning up behind the counter and didn't notice them at first. Kori was the first to speak. "So how'd it go today?" She walked behind the bar as Paige found a seat. A smile lit up on Janine's face.

"Not bad. Business is still going strong. Karen called and said she might be a little late. She's got something she needs to stay after school for. She's due in at five but she said no later than six. How was your morning?"

"Don't ask. Just one of those days." Kori had never taken much notice of Janine outside of a business aspect but today even Kori saw a smile born not of work but pleasure. Kori was about to comment but Paige beat her to it.

"That's an awfully big smile to wear for just work. Got something you'd like to share with us girls Janine?"

Janine's smile broaden just a bit. "Well, I met this guy online about six weeks ago.His name is Tom and he lives in Cleveland but we haven't had a chance to meet yet. That comes Saturday night."

Kori could hear the excitement in her voice but never liked the idea of blind dating. "How come it's taken so long to meet him if he lives so close?"

"He was in the middle of a divorce and custody fight. He thought it might look bad if someone saw us together before it was all over. And I have a favor to ask if it's not too much.?"

"Ask away."

"The only night he can get away is Saturday. I know we have the live music scheduled for that night but do you think I could skip out whenever he gets here? It wouldn't be any earlier than ten thirty."

"It's not a problem. Karen will be here to help clean up and Paige has been drinking enough lattes that she should owe me at least two hours of labor." Objections from Paige started almost before the words left Kori's mouth.

"Now just wait a minute. I'm doing you a favor here woman. I could be sitting in my bookstore driving my manager nuts or lounging on my sofa in my pink silk pajamas. And if I didn't think Bakker or Harding would kick my ass, I'd leave right now. So, does this mean we get to meet the online guy if we're here Saturday night?"

Janine nodded her head. "And if he's ugly I'm trusting that you two will say I'm not here."

Kori and Paige agreed unanimously they'd play along if they didn't approve. That had all three women laughing when Elliot walked in. He wore the same curious look Paige and Kori had seen on the detective's face earlier which just made them laugh harder.

Elliot just shook his head. "Sometimes I just don't understand women. What should have been a nerve-racking day has them laughing. I just don't get it."

Kori got control of herself and smiled at Elliot. "If I don't laugh, I'd probably cry. And that's like admitting this guy has won. How was your day anyway?"

"Besides the police visiting me, just fine. I didn't have much to do today. I called but you weren't home and figured you'd be here. I take it Paige has been doing her job of entertaining you and keeping you out of trouble?"

"Yeah. She's turning into quite a drag."

Paige turned to both of them. "Is this 'pick-on-Paige-day' and I don't know about it?"

"You know I love you. After twenty years I figure I'm stuck with you anyway."

"And don't forget it either."

"Forget what?" They all turned and saw Gabe walking in. Paige smiled and they all greeted each other.

"So what brings you to the cafe at this time of the day?" Paige was just as surprised as the rest of the group to see him.

"I told you the diner wasn't a difficult job. Took less time then I thought. Figured I'd stop in for something hot before I head home. So, what's new?"

The four of them spent the next few hours at the cafe chatting, discussing the case and listening to Janine talk about her date Saturday night. Karen came in at six and Janine went home. They all debated the issue of online dating but nothing was ever settled, whether it was a good or bad thing. But the storm grew and the winds pick up. And none of them would ever forget what would become of Janine's date.

CHAPTER 9

He'd worked for months to get to this day. By Saturday afternoon he could barely conceal his excitement but he had too. Almost to the prize ring. Since showing his superior work with the dumb blond three weeks ago, he could almost taste Kori's mouth on his as they kissed in celebrating two superior beings finally joining. He knew she was starting to understand him and that was definitely a move in the right direction.

He still wasn't sure how she felt about the first girl but he knew Kori understood why Boyd had to go. Boyd might have had ideas about getting back with her and that could never happen. She was special and only he could meet her needs. But tonight would be extra special. Kori wasn't surrounding herself with the right people and he had to show her the way.

He finished what work he had and went home to prepare for the evening. He'd thought it out very carefully. It took almost two months for the sacrifice to be hooked. Boyd had been an unforeseeable glitch but Shelly and the rest he'd known would have to be taken care of eventually. He desperately wanted to dress for the occasion tonight but he couldn't.

No attention would be brought to him until he was ready for it. He'd told her a time but he'd never intended to be there when he said he would. A phone call to say he was running a little late and she would wait. Just desperate enough to actually wait for her own death. He tried not to see it as simply death. It was like a new beginning for both of them. She could be rid of the body that tied her soul to this earth and he got to show Kori she should be more selective of her friends.

Glancing through his closet, he decided on a dark blue turtleneck, jeans and a sports coat. He wasn't particularly attached to the clothes so he didn't mind burning them if he got some blood on him. He'd have preferred clothes that weren't so binding, something that allowed him to move more freely, but he had to look as 'normal' as he could. So many missed his elevated statute.

It was approaching seven o'clock and his heart was beating a little faster. After tonight only two more remained and their demise would come quickly. Kori was able to brush off Boyd and knew she would weather this too. He'd watched her a few days ago after he'd called her. She continued to go to work and laugh and function. She was becoming used to him.

He knew the power inside him could be transmitted over cable wires. He knew Kori could not only hear him when he called but could also feel him. He checked himself out in the mirror and, relieved to see he looked as he always did, was then convinced his godliness had been covered just as it always is. But before his gifts to Kori die, he could see in their eyes not only understanding but surrender. It was the surrender of themselves to the better good of a new people.

New people. That's what he and Kori were. A new and different breed that belonged together. They needed no one and would support each other. And the sooner Kori learned how to live in a supreme realm that required only him, the better off she'd be. She'd be more accepting of him and to her own niche in that world. She would also be more prepared to face her fate with him. He knew it must be a daunting task to someone so blind as she, but he would show her the way. The only way.

Grabbing his wallet and keys, he headed out the door. A pit stop had to be made before the big date and for once he let himself drift to the past. He considered what he was doing a labor of love. He'd tried before and at the last moment the brass ring slipped from his fingers. He wouldn't fail this time. He wouldn't make the same mistake and let Kori go on not knowing her true path in life. Soon, the past would come forward and lead the future.

After the stress of Tuesday, Kori had actually been looking forward to Saturday. She and Janine had listened to the band that would be playing tonight almost a month ago. They had come into the cafe with only a simple drum set and three guitars and Kori hadn't had much hope for them. Surprisingly, they were good. They called themselves "The Railroad Cross Band" and did mostly folk music but Kori thought they could play well enough to hold the attention of the younger crowd. Janine wasn't as sure about the under twenty-five people until Karen spoke up and said she thought they'd do really well.

By nine o'clock the place was packed. On top of the regular customers that came in on Saturday's, 'The Railroad' had their own following. Kori and Janine were so busy making drinks, they had Karen take the orders and just yell them out. Elliot had been there since six and had taken his 'regular' spot at the bar. Kori was beginning to think he'd taken up people watching as a hobby. Paige popped in around eight and Gabe wasn't far behind. Kori wondered if they drove together and just entered separately or if they actually came on their own.

She struggled for a while with the memory of Poetry Night a few weeks ago. That was the last time they'd been together for an event except tonight, Boyd was obviously missing. But the crowds rolled in and she didn't have time to linger on the memory. Every once in a while she'd glance over at Elliot and he'd smile and she thought somehow he knew what she'd been thinking about. But life went on and there were drinks to be made.

At ten, Janine went upstairs were she'd left some clean clothes and freshened up. Ten thirty came and her eyes became glued to the door. Kori watched Janine while Elliot, Gabe and Paige watched the door with Janine. The band stopped playing at a quarter till eleven and people began to leave. Detectives' Bakker and Harding took a very secluded corner and were hardly noticed through the evening. A police officer was posted at the back entrance and one in the back office, just in case. Except for Janine's date not showing, the evening went perfect.

At five minutes after eleven Janine noticed a light blinking on the phone indicating a message had been left. She walked over, picked up the phone and listened to the message. Everyone at the counter noticed she was smiling the entire time. She turned to find all eyes on her. Janine grinned and said it was her date. "The volume must be down or we just didn't hear the phone ring. He's running behind. He said he'd be here closer to eleven thirty but that he would still be coming. Kori, if you want to go, I can close up. I'll be here for a little longer anyway. Why should you have to stay if I can close?"

Paige spoke up almost immediately. "And what if you don't like him? You're really stuck with him then."

"I'll just have a cup of coffee here with him and then tell him it's late and I'm tired and send him on his way. It's not a big deal."

Kori and Paige looked uncertain about the whole thing until Gabe spoke up. "Can't the detective's leave one of the police officers here until Janine leaves?"

Everyone looked at the two detectives standing by the door. Bakker shrugged his shoulder and said, "I suppose so." But Janine was already shaking her head. "So if I don't scare him off that surely will. How exactly would I explain that? 'Just in case you're some kind of freak, there's a cop watching me.' Not a good way to start things off."

Elliot suggested they leave the cop in the back but then Janine would still have to let him know she was leaving. "Couldn't he just listen for a car leaving?"

Janine continued to shake her head. "I don't need a cop on a date with me. Trust me. I'll be fine."

Kori had remained silent but finally had enough. "Okay. First, it's not you we don't trust. Second, I can see your point on everything so far. It's your call Janine. We're just concerned about your safety."

"And I appreciate what everyone's trying to do for me but I'm okay with this. Go home. I'll be fine. I'll call you in the morning."

Kori suddenly felt like the big sister. She walked over to Janine and hugged her. "Don't leave here if you don't feel comfortable with him. And you better call me in the morning." She let go, turned to Elliot and said, "Let's go home." Paige grabbed her stuff and headed out the door with Gabe in tow. Detective Harding held the door open for everyone and waited for Bakker.

Detective Bakker hung back for a minute and watched Janine.

Finally he told her to be careful and call the police if anything happened.

"I will." She smiled.

It was supposed to be a reassuring smile but something made him linger.

"I promise, cross my heart." She placed her hand across her heart and smiled again. Then, with a few flips of her hand, she dismissed him saying, "Go. I'll be fine."

Outside, Bakker and Harding watched everyone get into their cars and drive away. Harding watched for a second but found Bakker's face more interesting. Bakker felt him staring and turned to Harding. "What are you staring at me for?"

"Just wonder what your problem is."

"I didn't know I had a problem."

"Sorry. I just assumed since you're working those jaw muscles like you got a wad of gum in your mouth that you had a problem."

Jonah hadn't realized he was exhibiting his uneasiness. He often referred to it as 'the hunch' you always hear TV cops say they get. But his stomach muscles were working just as fast as his jaw was. He didn't like leaving a friend of Kori's alone this late meeting a complete stranger. "I'm going to leave Jackson in the back of the store."

Evan eyed Bakker. "Janine's not going to like that."

"That's why I'm not telling her." Jonah and Evan walked to the back of the store where the loading dock was. Officer Jackson was still parked there. The officer got out of the car when he saw Bakker and Harding approach. "Everything all right?"

Bakker nodded. "Fine. Listen, one of the employees is meeting a blind date here. The guy is supposed to be here around eleven thirty. Would you mind sticking around for a while?"

"I can stay. How long you want me to sit here?"

"Let's say an hour. That should be sufficient time. Drive around the front and see if they're still in there. Radio in if they've left or not. If they're still there I'll have a car drive by every half-hour."

He phoned the cafe to tell Janine he'd be there in ten minutes. He enjoyed making her wait and allowing the anticipation of the evening ahead to build inside him. He knew about the cop in the back but that didn't faze him in the least. Nothing would stop him tonight. His smile widened. He would do as he wished while a cop sat in the back. He couldn't have planned it better.

He waited till everyone had left and then pulled in front of the cafe five minutes later. He made sure all the buildings around the cafe were dark and nobody was walking anywhere near. Saturday night didn't bring much business to this end of Tabor. Most of the bars that the college kids frequented were closer to the college and the Movie Theater was on the other side of town also. But he had to be careful going in. And he had to move fast.

Once inside all his work could be done behind the bar and he never worried about the glass front. He wished he had more time to work with her but knew the last part of the evening might be difficult. He stuffed all he needed into a backpack, slipped it on, then pulled on his jacket. He knew she'd open the door for him but he had to get her mouth covered before she screamed. But that was simply a challenge to overcome.

Approaching the door he could feel the adrenaline pulse through his body. He was shaking with excitement. He had a wide, gray piece of electrical tape ready in one hand to slap on her mouth. He knocked and waited for her to open the door. He knew he had the element of surprise on his side.

As he watched her walk to the door, her smile faltered a bit and a frown creased her brow. A curious look came across her face but still she unlocked the door. He thought he heard her say 'hi' but couldn't be sure. He pushed inside the cafe and was on her and had her mouth taped before she ever knew what exactly happened. He dragged her behind the bar, threw her to the floor and sat on top of her. He punched her hard in the stomach twice so any ambition to fight would disappear with the pain and pinned her arms with his knees.

Pain and fear were the first expressions he saw but those gave way to confusion when he smiled and said, "Hi Janine. I'm Tom. You know, you should be more careful who you talk to on the computer." He waited for the look he loved to see. He slipped off his jacket and backpack and started pulling out his toys for the evening. He hadn't needed much and saw the fear come back to her face as he unpacked the rope, hammer, nails and drill.

"I am sorry it's come to this Janine but I have a lesson that needs to be taught here. You see, as long as you're around, Kori will continue to believe she needs you. And of course she doesn't. Kori is a very special person but hasn't learned that yet. She only needs herself and me, naturally. She can't depend on people that are beneath her." He talked while he readied his tools. He'd wanted to be a bit more dramatic this time and smiled as he imagined Kori walking in the cafe in the morning.

He'd given some thought to how he would accomplish his mission tonight. Once he thought of needle nose pliers he was in business. After attaching the bit to the drill he looked down at her. "You should feel quite privileged you know? You are part of Kori's salvation. I'm bringing her the knowledge to be free from mere mortals and closer to the godliness that she's unaware of." He pressed the trigger of the cordless drill and watched as the bit turned.

He could feel Janine start to twist underneath him. He watched as knowledge spread across her face and her nostrils flared as she began breathing harder. "Now don't be difficult. We both know what's going to happen here but we each have a role to play.

Shelly played nice and Boyd, well, Boyd fought but eventually realized it was a futile attempt. His girlfriend was quite spunky. Kind of like you." He adjusted himself so that his right knee stayed on her right arm and his left hand held her left palm. Janine's face now lay directly beneath his stomach as he arched over her. Looking down at her, he smiled, placed the drill two inches below her open left wrist and pushed the trigger. She thrust her body up and a muffled scream came from her taped mouth but by the time he felt the drill hit the wood floor, her body was limp.

He moved his knee and grabbed the rope and pliers. Putting one end of the rope in the tip of the pliers, he pushed the pair through the hole he'd drilled. It had worked perfectly. Two feet of nylon rope now ran through a hole in her left wrist. He could feel his pants soaking up the warm blood that was rapidly spreading beneath them on the floor. He hoped she lived long enough to see the end but wasn't sure. He repeated the procedure on Janine's right wrist. She moaned a couple of time as he pushed the rope and pliers in but never regained consciousness. Oh well. He was enjoying himself anyway knowing a cop was sitting outside.

Once her wrists were threaded, he pulled out a screwdriver and finished what he needed to on Janine's body. He then pulled two eyebolts from the backpack and hopped on the bar. Wooden beams approximately four feet apart ran the entire ceiling. He drilled a hole in one above the bar and screwed in the eyebolt. He moved down and screwed the second bolt into the next beam. Next, he picked up a tall bar chair and positioned it between the two beams. He jumped behind the counter and lifted Janine's body onto the bar, hoisted her from behind and propped her in the chair. He worked as quickly as he could knowing this was the most dangerous part. The lights were dim but if anyone looked in now they would see him.

He slipped the rope in the first bolt and tied a knot loose enough that once both ropes were tied in the bolts he could still tighten them. He got down from the bar and retrieved the hammer and one eight-inch nail. He pulled off Janine's shoes and socks, put one foot on top of the other and slid her feet back a couple of inches. It looked as centered as possible. He placed the nail on top of her feet and brought the hammer down twice till he heard the nail hit wood. He was certain at that point that Janine was dead because she never flinched or made a sound. That really was too bad.

He got back on the bar and stood behind the chair. He lifted the body and with his leg, slid the chair away from him trying not to knock it off the bar altogether. He rapped one arm around Janine's body, grabbed the rope and pulled. Repositioning himself, he did her other arm. When he was confident the ropes were tight enough, he let go of her. He jumped off the counter and stood in front of

Janine. Stunning was the first word to come to his mind.

He wished there was a way he could prop her head up but then he thought even Jesus had his head bent while on the cross. He pulled the chair down and packed up his toys. He took his clothes and shoes off and threw them in a plastic garbage bag and walked upstairs. He put on clean rubber gloves and rinsed off in Kori's shower and dressed in clean clothes he'd brought with him. He brought two large buckets he'd found upstairs and had filled with water and splashed down the floor and counter. He hadn't been cut so the police would find none of his blood and he'd worn gloves but he had tracked bloody footprints and he refused to leave those behind.

He left a note with Janine, grabbed his backpack and jacket and headed out the door. He glanced at his watch. All his fun had taken forty-five minutes. He threw his stuff in the passenger side, shut the door, walked to the drivers' side and got in and drove away. He couldn't wait till morning.

Karen was having the time of her life Saturday night and continued the joy into the early hours of Sunday. After she left the cafe, Karen went to spend the night at her girlfriend Tina's house which, in itself, wasn't all that exciting until she factored in that Tina's parents' were gone for the night. They had invited a few other friends over and partied until three in the morning. The house didn't look bad until everyone left. The living room was completely trashed and she and Tina cringed when they saw the bathroom. They decided to start cleaning right then and there while they still had the energy.

By five thirty in the morning the house was pretty well put back together. They were both exhausted and hungry and completely sober when they'd finished. It was Tina's idea to go out for food. "The only thing we have left in this house is cold pizza and stale chips. I need some real food."

"Tina it's not even six o'clock. Whose open for breakfast this early on a Sunday?"

"There's a Denny's open twenty-four hours in Newton Falls." She got her coat on and grabbed the car keys. "Are you coming?"

Karen followed right behind her. There was a bagel shop in downtown Tabor but neither of them could remember what time it opened on Sunday. Karen was almost certain it was eight but they decided to drive through town on the off chance they were wrong. As they approach the cafe, Karen frowned. She and her parents once went on a trip and had to leave early in the morning. They'd driven past the cafe and there had been low lights on but this morning it was completely dark. The sun had yet to rise and Karen asked Tina to slow down.

Tina slowed down and came to a stop in front of the cafe. "Something wrong Karen?"

"I thought lights were supposed to be on."

"Maybe Kori just shut everything off last night."

Karen couldn't imagine Kori deviating from the norm. If anything, Kori was a creature of habit and extremely picky when it came to the cafe. She guessed that if the business was her livelihood she might be a lot like Kori. Then she remembered Janine was supposed to close. "I don't think so Tina. I just can't see Kori doing that. Besides, I think Janine shut down the place."

"So what do you want to do? Call the cops? Maybe a light just burned out."

"Pull over and let me see if the door's locked. If it is I won't worry about it."

Tina pulled the car over and Karen got out. She tried to see in but the street lamps were casting a glow against the glass and making it almost impossible to see in. Her heart was beating a mile a minute and suddenly she didn't like being alone on the streets she'd grown up on. She grasped the door handle and pulled. She heard the soft chime of the bell at the top of the door and froze. Kori or Janine would never leave the door unlocked. Karen ran to the car, threw open the door, slammed and locked the door in one swift movement.

"You're freaking me out Karen. What happened?"

Karen tried to slow her breathing before she spoke out. "Got your cell phone on you?"

At first Kori thought she was dreaming about a phone ringing, but by the sixth ring she realized it was her phone next to the bed. In a sleepy voice she said, "Hello?"

"Kori this is Karen. I'm sorry to wake you but I had to call. Tina and me were driving by the cafe and it was all dark and then I went to the door and it was open. Did you forget to lock up last night?"

Karen was done speaking before Kori could register the name. Karen was calling her about locking the cafe up? "Karen, slow down a minute. Janine closed up last night." Kori was completely awake the minute the words left her mouth. "Karen where are you?"

"In Tina's car outside the cafe."

"Karen, listen to me very carefully. It may be nothing at all but I want you two to go to the police station and tell them what you saw."

Kori was up and dressing while she talked to Karen. After hanging up with her she dialed Detective Bakker's home number. Kori just got her second shoe on when he answered.

"Bakker."

"Jonah it's Kori. Something's wrong at the cafe."

"What do mean?"

"We always leave the recessed lights over the bar on at night. Karen was driving by and noticed the cafe was completely dark. She tried the door and it opened. Janine would never leave the place like that."

"What is Karen doing out at six in the morning and where is she now?"

"I have no idea what she was doing but I sent her and her friend to the police station."

"Alright. I'll be there in ten minutes. I'll let you know what happens. Just stay where you are."

"I don't think so." She hung up the phone before he could yell at her. Kori ran into Elliot in the upstairs hall. Looking confused he said, "Were you talking to someone? What are you doing up and dressed?"

"Something's happened at the cafe and I'm going over there now. I was just on the phone with Bakker and he's on his way there too."

"Let me throw some clothes on and I'll take you. You're not going alone."

Kori knew Karen and her friend made it to the station when she saw the entire downtown area lit up with red and blue pulsing lights from the police cruisers. She counted five before Bakker and Harding pulled in right behind her and Elliot. And she could see immediately that Bakker was furious with her.

"I told you to stay put."

"And I have a right to know what's going on with my business."

Bakker glared at Elliot, ready to tear into him but then realized Elliot probably didn't have much choice in the matter either. "Fine. But this is a possible crime scene, which means you go no farther. Where is the main light switch located?"

"Behind the counter. Left side of the espresso machine."

She watched as Bakker talked to the police officers there. One went behind the building, one stayed out front near her and Elliot and the three others lined up behind Bakker and Harding. They drew their guns and Harding pulled out a flashlight and clicked it on. She could see the flashlight being moved around and then an officer stepped out and approached her and Elliot. "Ma'am, the detective said for you to come with me to the police station." She was about to argue with him when someone turned the lights on inside.

Kori heard someone yelling in the cafe but what he said never penetrated her brain. The image her eyes were sending her was so incomprehensible it mustn't be real. It must be a sick joke somebody was playing on her. But from some place deep inside her she knew that what she was seeing in the cafe was horribly real. Kori momentarily noticed she somehow was kneeling on the ground but she couldn't remember going down. She heard Elliot talking to her and felt his arms around her trying to get her to stand up. The officer stepped in front of her to block her view and then she saw Bakker in front of her.

Kori could hear Bakker speaking to Elliot but his words were garbled. Elliot was pulling her in the direction of her car but her legs didn't want to work. "Come on Kori. We're going home now." Elliot's voice sounded strange to her though she didn't know exactly why. It wasn't until they were in the car that she looked at him and saw tears in his eyes and she knew the worst had happened.

Bakker watched them go and turned back to the cafe. He could still hear Evan tearing into the officer that switched on the lights before they got Kori away from the window. He didn't want to go back inside but he knew that was what they paid him to do. Jonah always figured no matter where he was a cop, he'd see murders but he'd hoped to be saved from the truly gruesome slayings that could occur. Apparently that wasn't to be his fortune in life.

Evan was quiet when Jonah walked back in the cafe. For a minute both stood staring at Janine's displayed body on the bar. He couldn't begin to imagine the suffering that beautiful woman went through. But he couldn't think like that. He lowered his head and started thinking like a cop. Turning toward the three officers standing behind him, he began barking orders.

"Nobody touches anything . I want this place picked apart, dusted and photographed. I want the coroner in here to give me an approximate time of death and someone get Officer Jackson here now. And I want statements and alibi's from Bowman, Hathaway and McCleary. And tape off the outside."

Jonah walked over to Evan who had moved closer to the body and was now directly in front of Janine. "That chair is soaked with blood. Looks like maybe he sat her in it at some point."

"What a sick son of a bitch."

"And I'd say it's our guy too. He left a note."

Bakker had overlooked it but he could just make out a piece of paper sticking out of Janine's shirt. As he remembered, it had been a light gray color when he left last night but now was discolored with blood. He exchanged looks with Evan and then decided. "I want this guy too bad to touch her."

Three hours later they had done just about all they could. They decided to concentrate on the area around the bar since they would get a hundred prints and fiber if they did the entire place. Bakker was more frustrated at the end than he was when they found Janine's body. The murder most likely occurred right behind the bar but it was, for the most part, clean.

Blood still lingered on the floor but it was apparent water had been poured there to clean any chance of footprints left. They found two small holes in the floor that probably came from the drill. Light drag marks on the counter suggested the bloodied chair was at sometime on the bar. Harding had the idea that the nylon rope may be the same used to tie Shelly Roberts to the tree so they bagged the rope and sent it off to an independent lab for analysis. Bakker knew the rope would be the same but what they found on Janine's body confused him.

He knew they would be lucky to find any physical evidence. Jonah even expected the note to be on the body somewhere. What he hadn't expected was what was above the note. The coroner, Tim Daniels, arrived twenty minutes after the call went in. He estimated time of death was somewhere between eleven-thirty at night and four-thirty in the morning. Bakker and Harding stood by the body until Daniels removed the note. Daniels handed Bakker the note, which had been bagged. Bakker started to read until Daniels called him. "Jonah. You might want to see this."

Bakker and Harding turned back to the body and saw Daniels holding Janine's shirt up. Just above where the note had been tacked to the body was a word scratched into Janine's body. In crude letters the word '<u>Salvation</u>' had been etched into the skin. Harding narrowed his eyes. "What the fuck is that?"

Daniels looked at the detectives. "Looks like your guy's got a god complex."

"Can you tell what he used to write that with?"

"I can almost see faint lines on the edges of the letters. This is only a guess until I get her on the table, but I'd say a Philips screwdriver."

Harding was shaking his head. "Thanks Tim. Jonah, let's go out for a minute."

Evan knew Jonah was about to explode. He could see his jaw

muscles going and they had yet to read the note. "Okay, lets get this over with. You want to read it or should I?" Jonah was still clutching the paper in his hand. In small, neat block letters another piece of poetry was written for them.

> Recollect the Face of me
> When in thy Felicity,
> Due in Paradise today
> Guest of mine assuredly-

"Kori's going to know he left a note Jonah. Do we tell her about the word he carved into Janine?"

Jonah shook his head. "I'm not sure where he's going with all this unless Tim's right and this guy's got a god complex too. I don't see what good it would do to tell Kori."

"Wouldn't a god complex still fit in with a narcissistic personality?"

"I suppose so. I just feel like we're trying to put a puzzle together and we're missing pieces. Like the corners that would hold it all together."

"Maybe we're not exactly 'missing' the corners. I think someone's just holding on to them."

"Well, whether missing or hidden, we need them now."

"You want to go talk to Kori?"

"Yeah. And her boyfriend too."

"Jonah?"

"What?"

"You talk to her about Bowman but I'd still like to talk to her about her ex- husband."

"Tyler Adams? You really think he's part of this Evan?"

"To some extent. Like maybe one of the corner pieces in this puzzle."

They drove over to Kori's and Elliot answered the door. Evan had to admit that if he was the killer, he put on one hell of an act. Bowman actually looked upset to him. "Professor. Mind if we talk to Kori?"

"Would you leave if I said you couldn't?"

"No, we wouldn't."

"Then come in. She's in the living room with Paige."

Elliot headed for the kitchen and Bakker and Harding walked into the living room where Kori sat with Paige. They both looked up when the detectives entered. It was obvious to the men that both Kori and Paige had been crying. Bakker cleared his throat and started talking. "I'm sorry Kori. And I'm sorry we have to be here now but we really need to talk to you."

"I guess I really don't have much choice."

"Can you tell us anything about the guy she was waiting for last night?"

"His name was Tom. Janine said he lived in Cleveland. I think she said he was divorced and had kids."

"Did she ever mention what he did for living?"

"I don't think so. How's Karen doing?"

Jonah hated sitting here talking to her. The pain on her face and in her voice was almost too much for him. And what made it ten times worse, is they really weren't any closer. "Karen's parents came and picked both girls up. She's shaken up and worried about you but I think she'll be okay."

"An officer has already been here to talk to Elliot. Are you going to question him more?"

"Not right now."

Evan saw this as his chance to bring up Tyler and jumped into the conversation. "Could I ask you a few questions Kori? About Tyler Adams if you don't mind."

"Detective, I've already told you I never saw Ty after I walked out on him. My lawyers handled all the divorce papers. I never contacted him afterwards and I never heard from him again. I've never heard anything about him since. I suppose that means he gave up on the singing career but that's only a guess. I don't know what else I can tell you."

"I know you can't add anything else to Tyler but old friends might be able to tell me something."

"I didn't keep in contact with anyone."

"It doesn't matter if you talked to them or not. They may have kept up with Tyler."

"I don't think they would. Tyler changed a lot after we married. He let the good fortune go to his head and in the end, even friends were getting turned off by him. I could tell you the names of the band members but I knew them by first names only. You have to understand, Ty wanted his home life and his career completely separate."

"Anything would be better than nothing at this point."

Kori thought about it for a few minutes but still didn't know how she could help them. Paige had remained silent until she surprised everyone with her idea. "Why don't you talk to Matt? He might remember something."

Evan turned and looked at her. "And how would Matt know anything?"

Paige lowered her head and spoke quietly. "A couple of days after Kori came back to Tabor, Matt and I had gone to his mother's in Newton Falls. I noticed some fliers around town advertising The Band playing at some bar. I was quite pissed at what Tyler had done and Matt must have been feeling protective at that time. Matt said he was going to the show and try and talk to him. I remember when Matt got home he wouldn't say much. If I remember correctly I think Matt's words were something to the effect that Kori was 'smart to get out now'. Like I already said, I was pissed and figured I really didn't want to know anymore than I did. Matt should remember that."

Kori was shocked that Matt had actually done that. Paige had never told her that story and it seemed so absolutely out of character for Matt. He wasn't the confrontational type at all. But she was even more confused why one detective wanted her ex-husband and the other wanted her current boyfriend. "Please try and explain something to me. Why are you two so interested in one man that had me and let me go and one that already has me? Why would Elliot or Tyler go to this extent for me? Or does this have something to do with a new note? He did leave one today didn't he?"

Bakker took a deep breath before he tried to explain his reasoning and to a certain degree, Harding's. "Bear with me for a minute okay? You and Professor Bowman have both admitted your relationship isn't a close, personal one. Is that your decision or his?"

"His I suppose."

"Yet he hasn't offered any reason as to why, has he?"

"No."

"But there is a reason we just don't know what it is. He has had opportunity in all three murders and to some degree, motive. That's assuming the motive is you. That's why we are also looking into Hathaway and McCleary. Opportunity and motive are there for all three of them." Bakker pulled out a piece of paper that he'd rewritten the poem on from Janine's body. He passed it to Kori and told her what it was. "The first line says 'Recollect the face of me'. I believe it implies that you know what he looks like because you know him. Since we don't know where exactly Tyler Adams has gone he obviously has opportunity."

"And his motive would be what Detective?"

"You left him and now he wants you back."

"After all these years?"

Bakker shrugged his shoulders. "It's plausible."

"I still think you're barking up the wrong tree. I don't believe any of your 'suspects' would do this to me."

"You may be right but then again, we may be right. It doesn't hurt anyone to look into them."

Kori wanted to scream at him. Was he kidding? It was damn near killing her that they thought Elliot would do this. It hurt Paige to think Matt could be responsible though she wouldn't admit it. And she knew it irritated Elliot that they thought of him as a killer. Instead, she offered the only thing she could. "I know you already know this but Tyler was from Cleveland and he did have two other brothers."

"Thank you Kori. I'll talk to you later. And I am very sorry about all of this."

Paige walked them to the door and a second later Elliot and Harley came in from the kitchen. Harley sat on the floor by her feet and Elliot sat down next to her. Paige came back and announced she was going home.

"I think I better give Matt a call and forewarn him I mentioned his name to the police again. I have no intention of another one of his visits. Besides, Gabe has probably heard what's happened and is undoubtedly chomping at the bit. Speaking of chomping on the bit, have you heard from your mother yet?"

"Not so far but I know I will. After Boyd's murder hit the news it took me two days to convince her to stay home and that I was okay. She'll probably want to move in with me now."

"Kori I love your mother dearly but I think that would push you right over the edge."

"Me too."

"Anyway, I'll give you a call tomorrow. Maybe we can do some more bonding ." Paige smiled and left the house. They both knew Bakker wouldn't want her alone again much less leave the house. She would have to do something about the quietness of the house though. Sitting with Elliot and Harley in the quiet let her mind drift and that wasn't a good thing. She saw the image of Janine on the bar and wondered how she could ever go back in there. She wondered how she would get through Janine's funeral. She wondered if she'd done something different, she could have saved Janine. Maybe she should have insisted on closing last night. Elliot put his arm around her and asked if she was okay. "Not really but I don't expect much."

"Kori it wasn't your fault."

"That's easier to say than to believe." Then she remembered what Bakker had said about Elliot's motive and figured she had nothing to lose by asking him.

"Elliot?"

"What?"

Kori hesitated for a moment knowing that his answer would change everything for them. She just hoped it changed for the better. "Is there a specific reason you don't want to sleep with me or is it that you just don't want that kind of relationship with me?"

Very softly he answered, "I have a specific reason."

Kori turned slightly so that they were eye to eye. "Between three murders, each one getting closer to my heart and you, I'm beginning to feel like the black plague. I think now would be a good time to hear your reason."

CHAPTER 10

Elliot knew this was not the time or the place for this conversation. He also knew that to avoid it would piss Kori off and he didn't think this was a good time for that either. Taking in a deep breath he decided to take his chances and avoid it one more time. He prayed he didn't screw things up.

"Kori you are not the black plague. And you are very special to me."

"But?"

He could feel her body tense and knew then she wasn't going to handle this well. "But I don't think this is the best time to discuss things."

She was off the couch and on her feet two seconds after the words left his mouth. "And just when the fuck is the appropriate time Elliot? Tomorrow, next week, next month or maybe after the next murder? I feel like I'm losing everything dear to me, including my sanity, and once again you don't want to let me in! Fine. You don't want me in on your little secrets, then I'll leave you alone with your thoughts."

She had reached the front door by the time he caught her. "Kori you can't just leave. I know Bakker wouldn't want you out alone. I won't let you."

"You know what Elliot? You don't have a choice if I leave or not. See that police car out there? I'm going to tell him to follow me if he'd like to but either way I'm going for a walk. And as far as Bakker is concerned, don't use what he would like or not like me to do. He's the one that thinks you're the killer remember? Bakker would just see me getting out of harms way."

Elliot listened to the door slam knowing there was no way to stop her. He watched as she walked over to the police car and then watched him slowly pull away from the curb and follow her. He'd never seen her quite this angry, especially with him. He'd seen her frustrated but not angry. Harley was standing next to him. If nothing else, Kori would come home for Harley. Now that he had just ranked himself below a dog he figured he'd go into the kitchen and see what he could cook them for lunch. Then again, Kori was really angry, he looked down at Harley. "Maybe we should think dinner instead of lunch."

Around noon he figured she went to Paige's since the cafe was off limits. He hoped she didn't go near the cafe and doubted if the cop car following her would let her or at least not let her linger. Elliot considered calling Paige and asking if Kori was there but if she wasn't Paige would probably lay into him worse than Kori had. Not that he didn't deserve it but that was his decision to make.

At two, Kori called to say she was with Paige but made no mention of coming home. When the clock chimed eight, he wondered if she would bother coming back tonight. He and Harley just got the wood burning in the fireplace when a knock at the door startled him. Kori was the only person he expected to see tonight and he suddenly had a sinking feeling inside. Slowly, he made his way to the front door. He opened it to Gabe Hathaway.

"Hi. Mind if I come in for a minute?"

"Kori isn't home right now."

"Yeah, I know. I was at Paige's house when she showed up. Pretty pissed at you right now. Anyway, I said I'd stop by and see how I could install a security system for her."

Gabe squeezed his way past Elliot and into the hall. Gabe started for the kitchen with Elliot entail. Gabe stopped and looked at Elliot. "You know, I think I can handle this by myself. I can yell if I need you."

"Security systems have always interested me so if you don't mind I think I'd like to watch."

Gabe studied him for a second. "Okay. Not all that fascinating but if that's your thing you're more than welcome."

They walked back to the kitchen and Gabe started checking out the windows and then the door. "I want to install a motion detector here, over the door. Someone even cracks the door and the alarm will go off." He opened the door and looked at the light. "I think a motion light back here would be a good idea too. What do you think Professor?"

"That's your job not mine. I'm simply observing. But what about windows?"

"I don't think the killer is sneaking in through windows. I'm sure he knows Kori has a dog and I'd assume he'd take the fastest, most direct route in. Don't ya think?"

"Again, that's your area. I was just curious."

"Well, I'll definitely hook up the front and back doors. Let's walk upstairs. Just to be on the safe side, I'd like to make sure there's absolutely no way in from upstairs."

They walked through the four upstairs bedrooms and bath. Elliot thought Gabe stood in Kori's room for more than necessary and finally said something. "If the killer isn't coming in through windows, what exactly are you examining in here?"

"Nothing." With that, Gabe turned and walked downstairs. He went into the living room and turned to Elliot. "So you mind if I ask you something?"

"That depends. What do you want to know?"

"If things aren't all that serious with you and Kori, you won't mind if I ask her out will you?"

" 'Things' as you say, are serious."

"Oh. I heard when Janine was killed your alibi consisted of you were sleeping on the couch. Doesn't sound serious to me."

Elliot could feel his blood pressure rising and his tolerance lowering. "That's between Kori and I and really isn't any of your concern."

"Uh, well, the way she was spouting tonight with Paige, I'm not sure you'll be around for long."

He flashed Elliot a full smile and for the first time in years, Elliot had the urge to knock out another man's teeth. "I doubt that but if it should happen I'll call and let you know."

Gabe could see he was irritating Elliot and that was good. Kori had been really mad and Gabe saw this as his way of protecting her.

Besides, if Elliot were gone, maybe Kori would have dinner with him. He had so much to explain. Paige would only see him as a fling and Elliot was the only thing stopping Kori from giving him a chance. "You won't need to call. I'll be there for her."

Elliot rolled his hands into fists and clenched his teeth. "If you done with your job, feel free to leave now."

"Well, actually, I thought I might wait for Kori."

"No, you won't."

"She did tell me it was okay to come over here. Maybe she'll be wanting my professional opinion."

"No, she won't. It can wait for tomorrow. She's had a very long day."

"Thanks to you. Now see, I would be cuddled in front of that fire with her, protecting and comforting her. Not letting her bitch to her friend on a cold evening."

Elliot had had enough. Quickly, he took one step forward and his fist connected with Gabe's nose. Blood poured out almost immediately. He hadn't actually been expecting it and the blow caught him off balance. Stumbling backwards, he hit the wall hard. He wiped at his nose and saw blood on his hand. Looking up, he smiled.

"Not bad for an old man."

Elliot's hand hurt like hell but he refused to register the pain for Gabe. "Now get out."

Still smiling, he turned for the hall. "I don't suppose I could get a towel or something?"

Elliot never answered him. He watched as Gabe got to the door, stopped and turned back toward Elliot. "I'm sure Kori will be impressed with your aggression. I bet she didn't know you had it in you."

Gabe walked out not bothering to shut the door. Elliot slammed it closed and cursed. He heard Gabe start up his truck but didn't leave for a few minutes. Elliot finally looked at his hand and saw a small cut that was bleeding. He must have hit one of Gabe's teeth.

He headed for the small bathroom off the kitchen and noticed Harley laying in the dining room. "Thanks for all your help dog."

Harley got up and followed Elliot to the bathroom. "I don't think you can help me now." Frowning, he said, "And why is it, every time the police are here or a confrontation breaks out, you leave?"

His hand had stopped bleeding but it had begun to swell slightly. Turning on the cold water, he stuck his hand into the sink. "You know he was right about one thing. Kori's not going to be happy I hit that asshole. Especially since she asked him to be here and I don't know if she wants me here." Harley sat watching and listening. Elliot was shaking his head. "And now I sound like Kori. I'm actually talking to a dog."

Gabe got to the end of the street and stopped the truck. His nose was still bleeding and he was beginning to worry it was broken. He never imagined the old man would really hit him. Maybe this was the catalyst Kori needed though. Maybe this would turn her off of Elliot. Kori deserved better. Though once she found out who he was, Gabe would be lucky if she even spoke to him, much less allow him to have any part in her life. He was about to finish driving home when he saw Kori round the corner. A police car was right behind her. She looked surprised and confused to see him sitting at the stop sign. She must have seen the towel he was holding.

Gabe realized how lucky he was that the cop had followed Kori instead of staying at the house. At least he would only have to explain the situation to her. She walked over to his side of the truck and he rolled down the window. She looked at him with concern and asked what happened. "I had a bit of a run in with your boyfriend. Sorry about that."

Kori was stunned by his words. "You mean Elliot hit you?"

"Well, yeah. I wasn't expecting it. We were just talking and he freaked out on me."

"Elliot 'freaked out'? Are you sure we're talking about the same guy?"

"Yeah. Well, I happened to mention that I wanted to have coffee with you and he got pissed. In a way it was my fault. Sorry."

Kori was still trying to process the image of Elliot having an enough emotion for her to hit someone over a cup of coffee. "No,

I'm the one that's sorry. Sorry you had to be involved in any of this. Go home and take care of that nose. Let me know how you are."

"I will. Take care Kori."

She walked away from Gabe more ticked off at Elliot than when she left earlier. This man had some nerve. As she went up the front walk, she heard the police car turn around and park on the street. Walking in the front door she noticed he hadn't bothered to lock it. Harley came padding down the hall to greet her and Elliot followed a second later. She saw a band-aid on his hand but she didn't care at that point. "Have you lost your mind Elliot?"

"Is that an actual question or are you being sarcastic?"

"I just ran into Gabe at the end of the street. You hit him?"

"He deserved it."

"He came over here to do me a service and you hit him and say he deserved it. I'm obviously missing something in this scenario."

"He wants to go out with you."

"And?"

Elliot knew he was on the verge of losing her. He had wondered if he'd blown his chance with Kori by not talking to her earlier and now he thought he did. "I didn't know we could see other people. Would you really go out with him?" Elliot prayed her answer would be no. But it wasn't a good sign when she didn't respond immediately.

Kori stared at the floor thinking about his question. She didn't necessarily have to think about it. She loved Elliot and knew it would have to be completely over with him before she even thought about dating anyone else. But he could wait for her. She's been waiting for him long enough he should know what it's like. "The way things are going between you and I right now, I don't know."

Elliot went into the living room and sat on the couch. "Could we just talk for a minute?"

"Elliot, I'm exhausted. Both physically and emotionally. I wanted to talk earlier and you didn't. I've had a very long day and right now I'd just like to go to bed."

He rubbed his hands down his face and brushed away the tears before Kori could see them. He got up and got his overnight bag.

"I'm going home now. I'll let the officer outside know that you're alone and they can send someone over to stay with you."

Kori was dumbfounded. He was actually going to leave right then and there. "So is this some sort of requirement for us? You don't want to talk and I leave and then I don't want to talk and you leave?"

He turned and looked at her and what she saw in his eyes made her heart ache. She wished she could have this day to do over. Hell, she wished she could have the last couple of months to do over. Elliot looked into her eyes. "I'm sorry Kori. I can't do this again. If you need anything just call me."

"I need you." It was the first thought that came into her mind. He had already turned to the door but he made no move to leave. She heard his words again and wondered what he meant. "And what do you mean you can't do this again? Can't do what again? We've never gone through anything like this before." Confused, she waited to see if he would answer her or just leave.

He spoke without turning around. "Seeing other people. We've never gone through this before but I have. With Sharon."

It took Kori a minute to register who Sharon was. "Your wife? When? While you were dating?" Again he made her wait for a response.

"No. About two years into our marriage."

Kori was shocked. Elliot didn't talk much about his marriage or life after Sharon but Kori had always been under the impression that he'd had a happy marriage. "Elliot I don't know what to say."

He finally turned to look at her and she wished he hadn't. The tears in his eyes were too much after today. "There is nothing to say. If you have doubt about what we have, then I'm not interested in keeping any of it."

"That's not fair Elliot. I can tell you right now that I love you. I have never doubted that I love you. You're the one that won't allow me to show you how much. You keep me at arms length. And now, after everything that has happened today, I really need you and you want to walk away!"

Elliot threw his hands in the air. "You want to talk and then you don't. You say you need me and then you run to Paige's. You say you love me but you can't say if you'd date Paige's handyman or not. Kori, what in the hell do you want? Do you know?"

"You know what I want? I want Shelly Roberts to be alive and in school right now. I want Boyd alive so that he could find a wife and start a family the way he wanted to. I want Janine working in the coffee shop right now. I want to forget what that maniac just did to Janine. I want the freak that's stalking me to be caught and held responsible. I want you. I want you to be able to put your arms around me and kiss me like we are more than acquaintances. When I walk upstairs I want you to follow me. I want to know what it feels like to lay naked in your arms at night. And I want to know exactly what the fuck happened with your wife! Does that cover everything for you?"

By the time she finished her whole body was shaking, her voice was racked with emotion and tears were streaming down her face. Elliot stood staring at her not knowing what to do first. He dropped his bag and stepped toward her. With one hand he gently wiped away the tears on her face and then wrapped his arms around her. Pressing the side of his face against hers, he lowered his head so that his mouth was next to her ear. Softly he said; "I love you. I've loved you since the minute I laid eyes on you and I've only fallen more in love with you as time goes on. Let's go sit down."

She knew he wanted to go into the living room but she was afraid to move. She'd waited for what seemed like an eternity to hear the words he'd just spoken and was scared to let the moment go. A few minutes passed and she released her hold on Elliot. They walked to the couch and she sat down facing him. Kori had the feeling he'd never told the story of his marriage to anyone so she sat patiently until he was ready.

Elliot took a deep breath and exhaled slowly. "Well, you know the basics. Sharon and I met in college. She was a year under me so we didn't marry until she had her teaching degree. I was just beginning my second year of graduate school and she was to begin teaching high school art class in the fall. We both understood since I still had at least one more year before I got my master's degree we would be living on her income alone. It wasn't until after I had my master's that the problems began.

"I was teaching at the local junior college after I graduated. I'd tried for positions in the English department at Tabor College but they were always looking for a doctorate degree. I told Sharon I was thinking about going back and getting my Ph.D. and just teaching evening classes at the junior college. I know she wasn't thrilled but she also knew I'd make more money with a higher degree. So that fall I began my doctorate program and taught the evening classes.
"We didn't see much of each other except on the weekends but I thought everything was going fine. It took two years but I got my degree and got an assistant professor position at Tabor that fall. But the position required me to teach one evening class and one weekend class plus one during the week. I was home for the most part during the day but gone a lot in the evening. The college was still on quarters instead of semesters so classes let out right before Thanksgiving and didn't start again until January.

"I noticed she had distanced herself from me but I chalked it up to our schedules. Once December rolled around and I was off, I thought things would improve between us. We hadn't slept together in about two months and when Sharon still showed little interest while I was home, I started to wonder if she still loved me. I tried to talk with her and promised that next year we would buy a house instead of renting one and start the family we both wanted. She had smiled and nodded alot and apologized saying she was just in a slump.

It was a week before Christmas that I got a phone call from the hospital. Sharon was in the emergency room. I flew to the hospital but they wouldn't let me see her right away. A couple hours passed and a doctor came to talk with me. He said she came in with vaginal bleeding and cramping . After examining her he said the other doctor must have used a dirty instrument or had a generally unclean exam room. Sharon had an infection and was hemorrhaging and it was safer for her to remove the uterus instead of putting her on antibiotics and playing a 'wait and see' game.

"I must have had a total look of confusion on my face because the doctor asked me if I knew what he was talking about. I had an idea but all I could do was shake my head. Thinking back, that doctor had to be horribly embarrassed. I'll never forget the look on his face when he told me that my wife had had an abortion. And we both knew I didn't know she was pregnant. He said Sharon told the nurse it was about three weeks since the abortion. He apologized again and said I could see her.

"When I walked in, Sharon wouldn't even look at me. I tried to remain calm but the longer I looked at her and the more I thought about it, the angrier I got. I finally looked at her and asked how could she know that it wasn't mine. It took her so long to answer I didn't know if she heard me. Still facing away from me, she said she wasn't sure the baby hadn't been mine. I wanted to die right then and there. I asked her why she did it then and she told me the other man threatened if she didn't have the abortion then he would come to me. Sharon figured the chances of it being my baby were slim and we could always have more.

"As much as I hated that she'd had an affair and had an abortion, I still loved her. I was angry for a long time but the anger was directed not only at her but also at myself. I thought if I had been less consumed with degrees and titles and paid more attention to my wife she would never have been driven into another man's arms. For a long time I didn't know if I wanted a divorce or not and Sharon changed a lot during that time.

"If I stayed out of indecision then she stayed out of guilt. Sharon never said as much but I know that's why she stayed. And I guess she figured if I was willing to stay with her even though we would never have children together then her staying was the least she could do to make up for everything. We never spoke about that day after she came home and I still wonder if she loved me or if it was just guilt that kept her.

"After that, Sharon didn't like to go to any doctor. When her stomach started bothering her she tried to diagnosis herself for months. I don't think cancer ever crossed her mind. It wasn't until she began vomiting blood that she went for a check-up. By that time, the cancer had eaten three-fourths of her stomach. I remember the day she died was the closest we came to talking about the abortion. She said she was sorry for the first five years but hoped she'd made me somewhat happy the last fifteen. I told her it was better than 'somewhat' and she smiled. The last thing she said before she died was that she was sorry she couldn't leave behind a part of her for me. I knew she was talking about children but I told her that twenty years of memories was enough.

"She closed her eyes and I held her hand until she died an hour later. I swore at that moment I wouldn't seek out another woman. I didn't want to love or be loved again. Until I met you."

Kori was in tears by the time he finished his story. She wasn't sure if she could even speak much less ask him the thousand questions she had.

"I'm sorry I never told you before Kori. It's not that I'm not interested in you or that I don't love you. It's never been about that. I just wanted to make sure that I was what you wanted."

She finally found her voice and could tell him what she had always wanted to. "Elliot, after Tyler and Boyd I knew exactly what I wanted. I found everything I wanted in you."

He leaned forward and gave her the gentlest kiss she had ever experienced. She hoped he would continue and he didn't disappoint her. He kissed her lips again and moved on to her cheek and then her neck. He pulled the back of her shirt lose from her pants and ran his hand across her back. Their lips found each other again but this time he let his mouth cover hers. There was a passion in him she never would have guessed and her breath caught for a moment until he pulled back and looked at her. He smiled at her and said; "If you walk upstairs I'll follow you." Kori had the urge to jump off the couch and take the stairs two at time but contained herself. She stood and slowly led the way to her bedroom. Her heart was pounding with excitement.

They took things slowly at first. Gently kissing and touching each other. They undressed one another with a seductiveness neither had done before. By the time they crawled into bed though, their passion had consumed them and it became more of an urgent need that had to be met. When they finished making love they were both exhausted but satisfied. They lay together, one naked body pressed to another, in a comfortable silence.

Kori guessed Elliot, like her, was lost in thought. She recalled all the 'wants' she had yelled at him and how he had met those that pertained to him. Kori understood her wishes for Shelly, Boyd and Janine would never come true but she hoped the monster responsible for their deaths would be caught soon. She thought of Sharon and wondered how a woman could do better than Elliot. In one way, she felt sorry for both of them. But she wanted so much to give Elliot what he wanted. A love that would never leave him. As hard as she tried to keep the thoughts of Elliot until she fell asleep, Janine and her death were what Kori remembered before sleep overcame her. What she would awaken to was worse than any thought imagined.

At first, Kori thought the pounding was part of her nightmare. She had been dreaming about Saturday night except that this time she told Janine to forget the date and go home. It was Kori in the cafe when the killer showed up and Kori was the one struggling to get free from the ropes that tied her. It wasn't until she heard Elliot calling her name that she slowly awoke. She was still lying in his arms just as she had been when she fell asleep.

But the minute she opened her eyes she knew something was terribly wrong. She sat bolt upright and the first thing she saw was Harley sitting in her doorway. It was barely audible but she could hear him whining. "Harley? What's wrong? Come here boy." But the dog never moved. He never even flinched to imply he might move. "What's wrong with you boy?" The memories of Shelly and the second note came flooding back to her. Harley hadn't moved then either. Elliot was sitting up next to her looking as confused as she was. "Kori?"

Kori did a slow once around the room. When she got to the mirror above her dresser she had to squint her eyes trying to compensate for the darkness. There was more pounding on the front door downstairs and the phone started to ring. Elliot grabbed for the phone as Kori jumped out of bed and ran for the light switch. Elliot was yelling at her to stay where she was and something about Harding on the phone but Kori ignored him. She threw a sweatshirt over herself and flipped the lights on.

Elliot was putting his pants on at the same time Kori saw the mirror. Harding was running down her hall, gun drawn. Elliot finally saw what had frozen Kori in place and she heard him whisper, "Oh shit.". Harding was yelling for them not to move and then saw that Kori and Elliot weren't moving a muscle and why. In small, neat block letters was a note written in what looked like lipstick on her mirror.

Each Second is the last
Perhaps, recalls the Man

Two lines were all it took to destroy any peace Kori had left. The monster had been in her room while she slept with Elliot. The invasion of her space was more personal than anything that had come before. The note she found in her hall was different. He'd been in her home but not a specific room and she hadn't been there. Kori thought this was one of the worst moments in her life until she heard Detective Harding.

"Kori? Elliot?"

"Detective Harding? What are you doing here?"

"Officer Jackson called into the station. Said he saw someone running behind the house. Go downstairs and wait for me. I want to make sure the house is secure."

"There's another poem on my mirror."

"Go downstairs. Now!"

Kori and Elliot headed downstairs and sat in the living room. Elliot wrapped his arm around her as they listened to Harding's footsteps upstairs. Five minutes later, he still wasn't down. Elliot went over to the window and saw the officer still sitting in his car.

"That's strange don't you think?"

"Which part are you referring too as strange?"

"That the cop is sitting in his car. Shouldn't he be looking around outside at least?"

"Elliot, I would think they know what they're doing. I haven't a clue as to what's going on right now other than a killer has been in my room with me in it."

Elliot turned and looked at the cruiser again and then back at Kori. "Kori?"

"What?"

"I think something is wrong."

"There is part of a poem written on my mirror which means the killer was in the same room we were and never knew it. I would say there's something wrong with this picture!"

Elliot was shaking his head. "I'm not talking about that. I mean with the officer outside and Harding still upstairs." Elliot swept the room with his eyes. "And where's the dog?" Elliot stood up. "I'm going upstairs to find Harding."

Kori was about to object until she heard Harding's voice. "I'm right here. No need to find me. Sit down, Elliot." There was harshness to his tone that made both Kori and Elliot frown. Elliot was still standing when Harding yelled. "I said sit down, Elliot. It's my show now." Harding brought his gun up and Elliot slowly lowered himself to the couch again.

Confusion blocked any other emotion Kori should have felt. Fear never factored in until Harding spoke again. "You see Elliot, you lose this time. Kori is special and deserves so much better than you. I tried explaining this theory to Sharon but she was weaker than I imagined. You don't get the prize this time Elliot."

Kori was trying to grasp the words Harding was saying but her head was spinning. She found her voice and tried working it out. "Sharon who? Elliot's wife?"

Harding smiled though there was no warmth to it. "Didn't Elliot tell you about Sharon? How she cheated on him? Got knocked up and killed his own baby? Or didn't you know that Elliot? See, I knew a long time ago I couldn't father a child but Sharon didn't know so when I threatened her to abort or have you find out, I knew the choice she'd make."

Kori now knew that Harding talking was the only thing keeping her and Elliot alive and she prayed Elliot was working on a way to get them out of this. She had to keep him talking. "How did you meet Sharon?" It was the only thing she could think to ask even if she didn't care one way or another.

"At college. We were in the same poetry class together. We got to talking one day and I said I wrote some of my own poetry and she asked to read it. Sharon loved it. I was a year behind her and she graduated and married before I had the chance to tell her how I felt about her. It wasn't until a year later when we ran into each other in the park that I saw fate intervening. "I asked how she was and Sharon simply unloaded on me. Told me her husband was either teaching a class or taking one and never had time for her. She said she was very lonely and wasn't sure what she could do to change things. I quoted her some poetry and she smiled. I asked if she wanted to take a drive and we ended up in a secluded spot. Actually Kori, you know the spot. It's right about where I sat with Shelly before I killed her.

"I was already a police officer so when she got pregnant it was easy to threaten her. She had no place to go. She didn't want Elliot to find out what we'd been doing and she knew she couldn't report the threat to the police. But she was weak. I thought she would clean herself up and come back to me but she didn't. She must have felt guilty and ended up staying with Elliot. It wasn't supposed to work like that. Sharon was supposed to be mine."

"Then this past spring I started coming into the cafe and met Kori. The more I saw you the more you reminded me of Sharon in some ways. You didn't just look at me, but through me, and I felt the special connection between us. And then one day I walked in and Elliot was sitting there talking to you. You were mine! Fate delivered you to me and I knew at that moment you would be mine."

"You were special but must not have realized. I had to show you that Elliot wasn't the man for you. I tried to show you the way to my love but you didn't see it and I don't think you do now. Don't you realize the extent that I would go to for you? Obviously not since you slept with him. I'm not sure you are the woman I thought you were. You seem to have chosen Elliot and that can't happen again. I won't let it. That's not the choice fate had for you."

Kori's brain was running as fast as her heart. She knew he wouldn't talk forever and Elliot hadn't said a word or moved a muscle the entire time Harding talked. "But Bakker will know it's you now."

"Not likely. Planning is the key to everything in life. All I needed was the perfect suspect to pin the whole thing on. I am surprised you didn't figure it out though. Gabe Hathaway is perfect. He's had access to you through Paige and it got better when he showed some interest in you."

Kori was now shaking her head. "But I barely know him. He has no motive to do this to me."

Harding's cold smile returned. "But he has the best motive in the world Kori. Didn't he even look familiar to you? He should have. He's your ex-husband's brother. I thought after you told Bakker and I about Tyler having a younger brother you'd have put two and two together but my luck held out. I hadn't realized you didn't know Tyler's brothers' name. Gabe somehow earned the nickname 'Jack' and that's how he was known. Oh, by the way, Tyler died about a year after you left him. Drug overdose but that's no great loss. Anyway, after I leave the last note Gabe will have a lot of explaining to do. You see, if you take the first letter of each poem it spells out Gabriel. Rather ingenious of me, I'd say."

Kori could feel the panic starting to set in and then she remembered the officer outside. "But if you shoot, the cop outside will hear and come to the house."

"Wrong again sweetheart. Officer Jackson won't be hearing anything. At least not in this lifetime."

Kori felt the coldness invading her entire body. The knowledge of what would most likely happen next registered deep inside her mind. And then for the first time she heard Elliot whisper one word to her and the horror it struck in her was beyond words. 'Run' was all he said but she knew exactly what he was going to do.

    At eight o'clock, Jonah had been at his desk for nearly an hour. And as the minutes ticked by and there was no sign of Evan, he was getting more than agitated. Janine's murder was front-page news in all the major cities. Someone had leaked how she was killed and his phone hadn't stopped ringing since he came in that moment. Evan had gone to the crime scene but should have been here ages ago. Jonah tried calling his cell phone around seven-thirty, got his voicemail and assumed he was on his way.

    By quarter after eight and no sign of Evan, Jonah dialed his number and once again got his voice mail. He slammed the phone down and yelled "Where in hell are you?". Jonah tried to remain calm and figured he would get done whatever he could. He really wanted to talk to the officer that turned the lights on in the cafe but after checking his notes, realized he'd never written the officer's name down. Evan had to have written the officer's name down somewhere.

    Jonah got up and walked around to Evan's desk. He was surprised to find Evan's notebook underneath some paperwork. Jonah couldn't remember ever having seen Evan without it much less leave it at work overnight. But he figured it was his lucky day because he knew Evan would have written down the name he was searching for. As he turned the pages he noticed Evan had copied each of the notes left for Kori. Jonah was a bit startled though to see how well Evan had copied the text of those notes. The small, neat block letters were almost the same as those left by the killer.

    Halfway through the notebook though, what Jonah, at first, thought was a business card, fell out. But when he turned it over he saw it was actually a card from a flower shop here in Tabor. And as the words, written in small block lettering, sunk in, his blood ran cold. As he was absorbing the sentence a call came blasting over the radio. Someone was screaming the police code for 'officer down' and then he heard the address being given. Seventy-five Maple Lane. Kori Chandler's house. Bakker knew in an instant Officer Jackson was not only 'down' but also dead.

Bakker was out the door and in his car in minutes. Jonah knew that if Evan had his radio turned on he'd know that he'd been discovered. Bakker ordered all officers' responding not to enter the house. It was too late to save Evan but prayed Kori was still alive.

Before Kori could say a word Elliot was on his feet, lunging toward Harding. Kori was up and running for the back door when the deafening blast of gun fire stopped her. But she knew the only thing she could do for Elliot was get help and that meant she had to get out of the house alive. In a split second decision, she started running for the door again. Kori had just yanked the door open and was reaching for the screen door when a hand wrapped around her ankle and pulled her down.

Harding was clutching the gun in one hand and her in the other but blood was coming from his mouth and she knew Elliot had gotten to him before the gun went off. She rolled onto her back and with her free leg, kicked at the hand holding her. Harding yelled and let go but both got to their feet in the same instant. He was right behind her as she ran out the screen door and then she felt his hand on her back. With one forceful push from behind, she lay sprawled out on the deck.

When Kori got up and faced Harding, he was blocking the stairs leading down. It was a twelve-foot drop over the railing and she knew she'd break a leg if she jumped. And then she saw him smiling again. Blood was covering his teeth and continued to slide out the corner of his mouth, which made his smile all the more horrible. "Looks like it's just the two of us now Kori. That's the way it should have been except not under these circumstances. You were supposed to be different. Special is what I thought. Someone that could see my intelligence and power and share that with me."

He took a few steps closer to her and she backed up until her back hit the railing. "I never expected it to come to this. You see I have no other choice but to kill you. I didn't have to kill Sharon. Before she left the hospital I paid her a visit. I told her the baby was

Elliot's and knew then that the guilt of what she had done would be more punishment than anything I could do to her. But you're different. You've really disappointed me Kori."

He raised the gun level with her head. "It should have been the perfect union of two special people."

Bakker's voice coming from below them in the yard made them both turn their heads. "Evan! You don't want to do this Evan! We can work something out!"

"It's over Jonah and we both know it. The only salvation is in death now. I knew that with Janine. I just hadn't realized it would apply to Kori and I."

Kori couldn't understand why Bakker didn't just shoot him until she turned her head back to Harding and saw the gun was still pointed at her. She was trying to figure quickly if she could make it over the side of the porch before he shot when a flicker of movement in the kitchen caught her eye. At first she thought it was Elliot until she saw the golden hair.

Before she could react she watched helplessly as Harley jumped through the screen, teeth bared. Harding swung around and Harley connected with him at the same time the gun went off. Stunned, Kori watched as the weight of Harley knocked Harding backwards and both went over the railing. Kori ran to where Harding stood only a second ago and peered down at him and Harley on the ground. She heard Bakker screaming and running footsteps coming from somewhere in her house but all she could do was stare at the two unmoving images on the ground.

CHAPTER 11

Two days after he was shot, Elliot was released from the hospital. He and Kori stopped by his home and picked up a few things before heading to Kori's. The doctors assured Elliot that the shot to his leg hadn't done any permanent damage and was expected to make a full recovery. He would need the aid of a cane for a while but that was a small price for what could have been. Harley came home the day after Elliot.

Harley had broken a front leg, two broken ribs and a bullet graze to his shoulder. And like Elliot, he was expected to recover fine. It had been almost two weeks after Evan Harding was killed before Kori heard from Detective Bakker. He was due to arrive at Kori's soon and the three of them now sat in the living room waiting. Kori and Elliot had spent many hours going over what Harding had told them and a million questions were left unanswered. They hoped Bakker would clear a few of those questions up today.

When Bakker arrived and Kori opened the door the stress of what Harding had done was clearly lined on Bakker's face. She smiled and he returned a very thin smile as she led him to the living room.

"Can I get you anything Jonah?"

"No, I'm fine. Thanks. I thought the least I could do was fill you in on everything that I can. I know you must have a questions. Harding kept a journal to some extent. Some of it is understandable but most sounds like the ravings of a lunatic. According to the journal, Harding picked out Shelly Roberts from the coffee shop. She had a set pattern and he followed her for a couple of months. Even talked to her a few times. I think, for once, that it was just a coincidence Shelly was also a student of Elliot's."

Elliot was shaking his head. "It doesn't seem like he left anything to chance. If he really didn't know then I'm sure it was that much sweeter when he found out she was, indeed, in one of my classes."

Bakker agreed with him. "In a sick way I suppose that's true.

Everything he told you about your wife Sharon though is probably going to be left as 'according to him'. He did mention Sharon's name a few times in the journal but never got specific with a last name nor does he go into any detail about a previous relationship with her. And even though I worked with him during that time, he never told me anything about it.

"Evan really did believe Boyd would try and get you back. At least that's what he wrote. We also never told you or the news, how the woman was murdered with Boyd. She was the one with him at Poetry Night. Dental records came back and gave us a positive ID on her and the picture her family sent sealed it." Bakker slowly shook his head. "She was a beautiful woman."

Kori was frowning as she stared at Bakker. "Why not tell me about her? Why keep her murder a secret?"

Bakker sighed. "For one, we didn't know who she was at first. She was burned very badly and it took weeks to get a dental match and notify relatives. Second, Boyd's murder was difficult enough on you. Third, when Evan called you and said 'two down, two to go', he wasn't even figuring in the death of that woman. I didn't think much about that until I was going over the notes this week."

"And how did Gabe get wrapped into all of this?"

"Paige McCleary. I don't think Evan planned to pin everything on Gabe Hathaway right away. By the time Evan killed Boyd he'd found Hathaway an easy target though. From his notes, Evan knew Gabe and Paige were sleeping together and he also knew who Gabe was. It seems Evan decided Gabe really wanting you would be motive enough for Gabe to be the killer."

"So Harding was just playing stupid when he would ask Kori about Tyler and his whereabouts?"

"Yes. Whoever placed the death notice for Tyler knew about Gabe and their uncle. I found the notice and it states that Tyler was survived by two brothers and an aunt and uncle, Keith and Margaret Hathaway. At first, he thought Gabe had been adopted because his last name was different. As Harding dug a little bit more he found that the Hathaway's never really did adopt Gabe. Gabe legally changed his name but those records aren't sealed like adoption records."

Kori was nodding her head as Bakker spoke. "We know about that. Gabe talked to Elliot and I a couple of days ago."

"Did he mention why he didn't just tell you who he was?"

"He said when he came to town he didn't know I lived here. The last time he saw me was in Newton Falls. Gabe had run away from home the night I met him. He said Tyler got quite nasty with him and Gabe decided right then that he wanted nothing to do with Tyler again. Gabe went back to his uncle and worked out the name change. When he saw the sign for the coffee shop he wondered if I was the same woman married to Tyler but I go by my maiden name. It wasn't until he was already working for Paige that he was sure."

Bakker understood where the story was going. And it would have looked stupid to tell you by then."

"Actually, he was worried more about people judging him. Sort of like 'guilt by association' I guess. He worried he wouldn't get business from people that knew me if they knew he was Tyler's brother. And Paige did admit, had she known, she probably wouldn't have hired him."

"Is he still working for Paige?"

"Yeah."

"Well, I think that about raps it up."

"Jonah, I'm very sorry about the officer you lost."

Bakker lowered his head and mumbled a 'thanks' and Kori knew not to pursue that line any longer. "I wish I could have solved this before he killed Janine."

Kori could feel the tears coming to her eyes. "I guess we'll all live with those wishes and some regrets for the rest of our lives."

Bakker stood to leave. "Elliot, I'm sorry I was so hard on you."

"You were doing your job. I understand that."

Kori walked Jonah to the front door. As he turned to leave he looked at Kori.

"Would you mind if I asked you one last question?"

"Not at all."

"Are you going to reopen the cafe?"

"Eventually. I don't think I could go back right now. Gabe has offered his services to do some remodeling."

"Just my opinion but I think that would be a service you should take."

"I think I just might. I do have one more question."

"What's that?"

"Harding mentioned another note he planned on leaving. What did it say?"

Bakker had anticipated this and had written the poem down on a piece of paper which he now handed to Kori. 'I hide myself within my flower, That fading from your Vase, You, unsuspecting, feel for me- Almost a loneliness.'

"It was written on a card from a flower shop."

"Thank you." Kori handed the paper back to Bakker.

She hugged him before he could turn away and thanked him again. She walked back to the living room and sat with Elliot. She couldn't remember the last time an hour had gone by that Elliot hadn't asked her how she was and he didn't disappoint her now.

"Are you okay Kori?"

"I think so. I know none of us will ever be quite the same and we've lost a lot but some good has come from this."

"Like Paige staying with Gabe?"

"I think she should have taken a break after Matt, but if Gabe makes her happy, then I'll trust she knows what's best. Besides, if Gabe is going to remodel the cafe I'm sure Paige will have a hand in that too. And it's not just Paige and Gabe that's good. Harley will be fine and you and I are also good."

"You're just saying that because I live with you now."

"And because I'm going to marry you." Kori smiled as she looked at the ring he'd given her. Elliot had convinced Paige, of all people, to drive him to a jewelry store yesterday and Elliot had asked Kori to marry him last night.

Elliot wrapped his arms around her. "Yes, that's a very good thing."

"I did forget to ask you something."

"What?"

MANIPULATING FATE

"How do you feel about children?"
Elliot smiled. "Can't wait to have them."
Kori snuggled closer. "My mother is going to love you."

Printed in the United States
17502LVS00001B/337-387